HOPE'S HONOR

KAY P. DAWSON

INTRODUCTION

Hope's Honor is Book 4 in my Oregon Sky Series. It can be read as a standalone, however if you'd like to read the first 3 books, where you will be introduced to some of the characters you will read about in this story, you can find them listed on my website...https://www.kaypdawson.com/oregon-sky-series

HOPE'S HONOR

Left in the care of her vindictive step-mother after the death of her father, Hope is shocked to find out the debt he's left them in. However, that's nothing compared to the horror she feels when she finds out how her step-mother intends to pay off that debt without losing any of her luxuries. With a little brother who has been deaf since birth, Hope has no choice but to go along with it to protect him.

Logan Wallace has travelled to Sacramento to purchase the cattle he needs to start his own herd, only to be greeted by a pick-pocket shortly after he arrives. Chasing the thief, he's led into the slums of the town where he's shocked to see some kind of human auction happening.

When his eyes meet the terrified brown ones staring back at him from the wooden platform, he knows he can't walk away and leave her there to the fate of the men who are bidding.

Putting up the money he was supposed to use to purchase a prized mare for his sister Ella, he steps in to help. But when he wins the auction and tries to let the girl have her freedom, he's shocked to find out that her honor won't allow her to walk away until she's paid him back in full.

So now what is he supposed to do with her?

CHAPTER 1

"*Y*ou won't get away with this, Sadie. If you think I'll just quietly go along with your plan, you're even crazier than I thought."

Hope shook as she tried to get her anger under control. The woman in front of her only sneered and laughed back at her.

"You have no choice, my dear child. You're still under my care, or did you forget that? When your father died, God rest his pitiful soul, you and Max were left with me as your only guardian. And since you're not yet eighteen, I'm still in charge of both of you."

Clenching her teeth together hard, Hope fought the urge to reach out and slap the other woman. Her stepmother had never liked her, only treating her kindly when her father was around. But when he wasn't, Sadie treated her brother Max and her like nothing more than slaves.

"I will be eighteen in three weeks."

Sadie just shrugged as she continued to laugh. "Well, that's three weeks too late, I'm afraid."

Hope turned to leave the room. "I'll be packing my things and taking Max. I'm not staying here with you another moment. I don't care if I'm not of age yet. We'll manage just fine on our own."

But before she could get to the door, her step-mother's words stopped her dead in her tracks. "I thought you might say that. And you're welcome to try leaving. However, just remember, if you get caught, things can get a whole lot worse for you. I'm the only person keeping Max from being sent to an orphanage. You aren't legally able to be his guardian. And I'm sure we both know how well a deaf child would make out in an orphanage on their own, especially when I can send him where you'd never be able to find him again."

Swallowing the fear that rose in her throat, Hope turned back and met her stepmother's laughing stare.

"I'll just have to make sure you don't find us until I'm of an age to be his guardian." Even as she slowly said the words out loud, she knew deep down that Sadie had already taken measures to make sure they couldn't run away. The smirk on the woman's face left no doubt.

"I guess we'll know soon enough what will happen." Sadie stood up and rubbed her hands down her skirt, smoothing the wrinkles out. "The auction is tomorrow morning, and I have no doubt you'll be walking up on that platform."

"You can't do this, Sadie. It's illegal." Her heart pounded so loud in her ears, she was sure it echoed across the room.

"I don't care what it is. The fact is, your father left me with no choice. I have no money, and the debt he left me with has to be paid. I don't intend to sell any of my jewelry or anything else I have. Those are mine. The man I spoke with about the auction has assured me there'll be so many men bidding on you that I'll have more than enough to pay the debt off. And have plenty to spare. It'll hold me over until I can find someone to step in and take your father's place."

Hope swallowed against the panic raging inside her. "What kind of person are you, that you'd put a young girl up for auction like this?" She could barely get the words above a whisper.

"Oh, for goodness sake, Hope. It's not like I'm sending you to the gallows. These men are merely looking for some help around the home. I've been assured it will be nothing more than a year of your life. In exchange, all you'll have to do is take care of their homes. Once the year's up, you'll be free to go."

Hope shook her head in disbelief. "Do you truly believe that's all they'll want from me? A man who attends an auction like this, bidding on a woman, isn't the type who'll be content with just having a paid maid around his home. You know that."

Sadie shrugged as she walked toward her. "Once I've got my money, it really is out of my hands." The woman brushed past her, heading out the doorway of the parlor.

"What about Max?" Her words were shaky as she struggled to hold herself together.

Sadie turned slowly and faced her. "If you co-operate, I've arranged it so that whoever wins you, knows he goes with you. But if you don't, I'll make sure you never see your brother again."

Watching her whip back around and leave the room in a flurry of velvet skirts, Hope's legs gave out as she sunk down onto the settee. A month ago, she'd been happily going through life without a care in the world, believing money would never be a problem.

Now she realized how naive she'd been. Her father had died, and without even having time to grieve, she'd been forced to face the harsh reality of what her stepmother had planned for her.

Tomorrow, she was going up for auction.

And she had no one in the world to turn to for help.

It was a shock to find out their father had left them with nothing. The wealth she'd always believed they had wasn't what it seemed. And Sadie had made it clear she was determined not to go down with the debt he'd left them in. Her father was barely in the grave and already Sadie was looking for his replacement. She'd made sure she'd be well looked after.

It didn't matter what happened to Hope or Max.

Hope knew the woman had never had any feelings for them and that she'd only married Hope's father believing he was wealthy. That was all that mattered to her.

Hope's eyes moved to the window and her heart lurched as she saw her younger brother bent over gently touching a butterfly resting on a flower. Max was her whole world, and he desperately needed her. He'd been born deaf, something that made life incredibly difficult for him to manage on his own.

Her parents had been overjoyed to have a son born to them. In the beginning, no one suspected anything was even wrong. But after it became apparent the baby couldn't hear, everything had changed. Hope had become fiercely protective of him, trying to shield her younger brother from the dangers of the world.

Her mother had spent countless hours reading books about how to communicate with a deaf child as he grew, and Hope had learned along with her. Their father hadn't had much interest in learning—his disappointment in having a disabled child was now evident in how he'd treated his son. He'd taken to spending his nights out drinking and gambling, while their mother had quietly continued to learn on her own.

Watching Max pick the flower carefully, with the butterfly still sitting on the petals, a tear made its way down her cheek. Her heart still ached for her mother, who had died from pneumonia over four years ago, leaving them with a father who didn't care anymore. He'd married Sadie to have someone to look after the children he'd been left with, but it was clear early on that this wasn't a job she was willing to accept.

Hope had been forced to grow up quickly and take care of her brother.

And it was a job she would never give up. It was a risk trying to get away from what Sadie had planned, but she had to try.

She couldn't just let herself be auctioned off, and hope the man honored the agreement to let Max come too. Somehow, Hope knew if she didn't at least make an effort to get away, Max would end up in an orphanage far away from her anyway.

Sadie might think she'd already won, but Hope wasn't giving up just yet.

As long as she was breathing, she'd do what she needed to keep her brother safe.

CHAPTER 2

S he sat on the edge of the bed, moving her hands like she'd been taught, trying to explain to Max what they were going to do. The house was quiet now, and the darkness of the room was broken only by the small lantern next to the bed. As she always did, she whispered the words to herself as she signed.

"Everything will be all right, I promise. Just stay with me, and if someone finds us, I want you to run. Run as fast as you can, and get yourself to Camille's house."

Camille Larsen was Hope's best friend, and the only one who knew how bad things were since Sadie had shown up in their lives. She also knew she could trust Camille to help Max. Her friend had always shown an interest in learning at least some of the sign language to communicate with Max, so she'd hopefully understand what he was telling her if he needed her help.

If not, Max could write it out for her. He was ten-years-old, and even though he still struggled with spelling sometimes, he'd learned at a young age how to communicate on paper.

Max's eyes were large in the dimly-lit room as he stared back at her. "But what about you?"

Hope smiled at the concern he showed in the words he signed back to her.

Shaking her head, she continued to explain, "Don't worry about me. If Sadie catches me, I'll have to face the auction. But if I know you're safe, at least I won't have to worry. As soon as I can get away, I will. And I'll come find you."

Max lifted his arm to quickly wipe at the tears forming on his cheeks. His face went into the stubborn scowl she recognized so well. "No! I'm not just going to let them take you," he signed.

Patting his hand reassuringly, she tried not to let him see the worry she was feeling. "It will be all right. If we're careful, we might not even get caught. Once we get away from here, we'll hide until I figure out where to go."

Taking his hand in hers, she stood and reached

for the small bag he'd hastily packed. When she'd come into the room to explain everything, he'd already been sound asleep, completely unaware his life was about to change so drastically.

She desperately hoped her brother couldn't sense the fear she felt as they silently made their way down the hallway to the door. A noisy floor-board suddenly creaked beneath his feet, seeming to vibrate against the walls of the house. Turning back, she put her fingers to her lips. The look of terror in his eyes broke her heart. With everything she had, she wanted to stop and take him in her arms, to reassure him everything would be all right.

She was sure he didn't really understand what was going on. All he knew was that Sadie was threatening to "sell" his sister, and they had to get away.

Hope wished she could shield him from the truth of the situation. But one thing she'd learned about Max over the years, was to never underesti-mate him. He was capable of understanding things much better than people ever gave him credit for.

Carefully opening the door, Hope peeked out into the darkness. She had no doubt Sadie would have done everything she could to make sure they didn't get away, so the fact the door opened so easily caused her some alarm.

But she didn't have time to think about it. They needed to keep moving. She had to get Max outside where he could make a run for it if he had to, then she'd at least know he was safe for the time being.

She stepped out onto the front porch and glanced around, checking under the glow of the street lamps and behind any bushes to make sure no one was watching. The sound of a wagon rumbled past the house, making its way toward the livery up the street.

They moved to go down the stairs, and she held Max's hand firmly, giving it a gentle squeeze to reassure him everything would be fine.

Suddenly, a hand wrapped around her, pulling her into a broad chest as the other hand came up to cover her mouth. In horror, she watched as Max came out from behind her and tried to kick at the man who held her in his grip. Another figure appeared from the other side of the steps, moving toward Max.

Even without hearing him coming from behind, Max seemed to sense the other man. He whipped around, and as he did, his eyes met Hope's. "Run," she signed.

He looked torn, not wanting to leave her behind, but probably knowing he was no match for the men in front of them. Just as the other man was about to grab his arm, Max quickly jumped over the edge of the steps and started to run.

She'd always known her brother was fast, but as she watched him now, she could see there was no way anyone was going to catch him. Her relief was short-lived though as he darted in front of the wagon that had been going past. It was well up the street by now, and she cringed as the horses reared up slightly and stepped to the side.

A sob caught in her throat as she held her breath, hoping to see Max come out from the other side. A man riding in the wagon leaped down and ran to the front. And just when she was sure she'd pass out from the pain in her chest, she spotted his small figure running in the other direction. The man from the wagon called after him, but she couldn't hear what he said. He couldn't know Max wouldn't hear him either.

"Quit fighting, Miss, or I'm gonna have to hurt you." Hot breath hit her skin as the voice hissed in her ear. The man who'd been chasing Max had moved back into the shadows when the wagon had stopped. And since the wagon was still sitting there in the middle of the road, it was obvious the man didn't want to take any chances of being seen.

She hoped it would be enough time for Max to get away and hide.

While she was dragged back into the darkness of the house, she tried to bite the man's hand. As she struggled against his hold, a shiver went up her spine when she heard Sadie's laughing voice behind her.

"You foolish girl. I told you I wasn't going to just let you go. You always thought you were better than me, and knew more than me. Well, now you'll pay. And you better pray we don't find your brother, because he's going to suffer for what you tried to do here tonight."

Sadie moved into the shadows of the open doorway. Flicking her hand in Hope's direction, the woman sneered at her. "Take her back to her room, and make sure you stand right at her door so she doesn't try anything else. Try not to rough her up too much—she has to look her best on the auction block tomorrow."

The woman looked out the door before slamming it loudly in the quiet of the night. When she turned back to face her, Hope was sure she'd never seen such hatred in anyone's eyes before. "It's a dark night out there for any young boy out on the streets of Sacramento by himself. Especially one who's deaf." She came closer and clicked her tongue. "It's a shame you just let your own brother out into the mercy of the city streets because you couldn't follow a simple order."

Sadie's laughter could be heard long after she walked away and back up the stairs to her own room. The man who held Hope started to drag her down the hallway, pulling on her hair as they went.

She knew she had to get away. This was her last chance. Twisting quickly, she managed to free herself briefly from his grasp.

But before she could get far, he yanked her back by her hair. He slammed his other hand into the side of her head with such force, she was sure she was seeing stars.

When they got to her room, he threw her inside onto the floor. As she sat crumpled among her skirts, his voice reached her ears, and his words shook her to the core.

"I pity the poor man who wins you tomorrow, unless he can teach you some manners and keep you in your place."

The door slammed behind him, and she brought her hands up to cover her face as the tears flowed freely down her cheeks. Her eye throbbed with every beat of her heart, reminding her of the treatment she was likely to be faced with for the next year of her life.

Tomorrow, she'd be auctioned off to the higher bidder, and there was nothing to stop the man who won her from treating her exactly like she'd been treated tonight.

Or even worse.

CHAPTER 3

"The cattle are all set and ready to make the trek back to Oregon. I've hired a few men to help us out, and Luke has agreed to come along with us to lend a hand." Logan Wallace lifted his foot to rest it on the wagon's top rung. James O'Hara, the older man who'd made the trip to California with him, was looking through the supplies he was adding to the wagon bed.

"It'll be good to see young Luke. I know Phoebe and Grace will be happy to see their brother." He lifted his eyes to look at Logan. "Any word on Connor?"

The youngest Wallace brother, Connor, had come down to California with Luke Hamilton to pan for gold. He'd said he needed some adventure in his life, away from the farm and homestead in

Oregon. Luke had agreed to keep his eye on the boy and they'd spent the past year drifting around down here.

Since Logan's brother, Colton, was married to Luke's sister, Phoebe, they'd all known they could trust the man to take care of one of the family.

But when they'd met up yesterday, Connor had said he wasn't ready to go home. He was learning to be a blacksmith and taking his training with a local man. Logan was proud that his younger brother was perhaps now ready to grow up.

"Have you got all the supplies you were picking up? I'm sure you can't fit any more in the wagon." Logan shook his head and chuckled as he looked around at the back of the wagon that was full to the top. "Lucky, I was able to find a chuckwagon and cook willing to come on the trip. There's no way we could have put anything more in here."

"Now you know the only reason I offered to bring you down here in my wagon is so I could pick up some much needed supplies for the mercantile back in Bethany." James grinned across at him as he tightened a rope that was holding some of the items in the back.

The truth was, James O'Hara had been a close family friend of the Wallace's since they'd arrived

in town. They owned the mercantile, and Logan
had known how badly they were hoping to get
some better supplies available to them in their
small town. When Logan had decided he was
coming down to California for his cattle, he'd
asked James to come with him.

It actually would have likely been easier for
Logan to just ride down on his own, but he knew
James would never have made a trip down here by
himself. So he'd made it seem like he needed some
help to bring his cattle back to Oregon.

Logan dropped his foot and moved over to help
the older man tie the canvas at the back. "Now, I
just need to meet with the seller who has that mare
Ella wants me to pick up for her. I'm supposed to
meet him up at Rosie's Saloon at noon. Hopefully,
we can be back on the trail and headed home by
tomorrow morning. I like Sacramento, but it
doesn't even come close to Oregon." Logan let his
eyes move around the crowded street, taking
notice of the dust that hung in the air as wagons
bounced past. Everywhere he looked, he could see
people walking, kids running, and what seemed to
him to be a whole lot of commotion.

He was used to the more quiet and laid-back
bustle of Bethany. The little town had grown a lot

in the past few years, but it was nowhere near as busy as what he was seeing on the streets around him today.

Suddenly, he was pushed from behind, making him lose his balance. Turning to confront whoever had bumped into him, his eyes fell on the top of a small head covered in black hair as it darted past.

Before the young boy could make it to the other side of the wagon, Logan spotted something else out of the corner of his eye gripped firmly in the child's hand.

"Stop! That thief just stole my wallet!"

Leaping out onto the street, he didn't even wait for James to follow. He knew the older man wouldn't be much help anyway. But if that vagrant child thought he was going to get away with stealing his money, he was sadly mistaken.

He was carrying the cash he needed for Ella's horse, so it wasn't just a few bills being carried off. It was a large amount of money and he knew his sister well enough to know she wouldn't be happy if he came home with no horse or money to give back to her.

As he raced after the boy, he vaguely noted the people he passed. No one seemed too concerned about a pickpocket and a man chasing after him to get his money. Apparently in the city, this was such a common occurrence it didn't even warrant anyone taking notice.

The boy never looked back, continuing to run as fast as his small legs would take him. And Logan had to give it to him—the kid could move. He was struggling to keep up as they wound past old buildings that looked like they were about to fall down with the smallest breath of wind, and into alleys that were so closed in, they were shrouded in darkness.

He knew he was getting farther away from the civilized end of the city and was most likely running into a situation far more dangerous than the loss of his wallet.

But he couldn't let the thief get away with it, even if something deep in his gut reminded him that if a boy was having to steal money, there was likely a good reason. Perhaps he was an orphan, or had a sickness in his family. Who knew what the kid's story could be?

Whatever it was, it didn't matter now. Logan wasn't the type to just give up, especially not when he'd come this far. And not with the amount of money the boy was now fiercely clutching in his hands as he ran.

His lungs burned as he struggled to keep up. It seemed like the boy didn't have any fear of being hit by passing wagons as he raced across the busy streets, with people yelling down at him in anger. Logan wasn't so quick to run out onto the streets, and was having to make his way more carefully, checking first to see what was coming so he wouldn't be hit.

Finally, the boy darted behind an old building and headed down a dimly-lit alley. It looked like there was no way out at the other end.

"I've got you now!" His words were more like a hissed whisper as he strained to catch his breath.

The boy ran to the left, and through a door that looked like it was holding on by only one hinge. Logan slowed down as he approached the doorway and tried to ignore the feeling of dread that was rumbling in his stomach. He'd run quite a few blocks chasing the thief, so if something happened to him down here, he wasn't sure James or anyone else would ever be able to find him.

Hearing voices on the other side, he carefully pulled the door open to assess what he was walking into. It was a small tavern by the looks of it, and it was packed full of the most unseemly-looking men he'd ever laid eyes on. As he stepped carefully inside, however, he noted there were a few heavily made up women too. They were making their rounds, stopping at tables and laughing with the men who paid them attention.

He knew exactly what kind of place he was standing in, and it made him feel sick. What would a young boy be doing running into a dump like this?

His eyes were having a hard time adjusting to the darkness and smoke that hung in the air around him. The smell of unwashed bodies tightly pressed into the small room made his stomach coil.

Finally spotting a small figure pressed up against a wall on the far corner, looking down at the wallet in his hands, Logan moved slowly toward him, not wanting to scare him off. The boy had likely figured he wouldn't follow him into the dilapidated building, so he wasn't paying any attention.

Reaching out, Logan grabbed the boy's collar, pulling him back toward him before he could get away. "I believe you've got something that belongs to me." He kept his voice low, even though he was sure no one around them was taking note of what was happening. They all seemed focused on the small platform at the front of the room where someone was being led out.

Did she have her hands tied?

What kind of place was this?

Looking back down at the boy he was holding by the scruff of the neck, his breath caught as he saw the tears in the blue eyes staring back at him. The child looked terrified, and didn't look like he belonged in a place like this at all.

Something was going on but Logan couldn't quite figure it out.

"What's going on here? Where are we?"

The boy just stared back at him, his small chin starting to quiver.

"I asked you a question, and if you don't want me dragging you off to the nearest constable, you better answer me."

He watched the muscles in the child's face crumple as the tears started to fall. The boy shook his head slowly, and looked down at the ground. He thrust Logan's wallet back at him and put his own hands into the pockets of his pants. His shoulders drooped and he looked like the world had just ripped the last bit of fight out of him.

Suddenly, he remembered a young boy running in front of him last night as he'd come back from meeting with the men he'd hired to help him bring the cattle back to Oregon. Bending down closer, he reached out and lifted the face back up to look at him. Squinting his eyes together, he took a closer look.

"You're the boy I almost hit last night. You looked like you had the devil on your heels. What were you doing out on your own? And why are you all the way down here now?"

The boy slowly lifted his hands and moved them in some kind of motion in front of him. Then he shook his head again and pointed at his ears. His young face was a stark red color where the tears had stained his cheeks.

He moved his mouth, but no words came out.

Logan finally understood what he was telling him, and guilt slammed into his chest like a stampeding longhorn.

The boy was deaf.

He loosened his grip on the boy's collar, but didn't let completely go. He wasn't the kind of man to just leave a boy alone in a place like this, especially not one who couldn't hear.

Looking around, he tried to see if there was anyone this child could possibly belong to. The men standing around left him hoping there wasn't anyone here who could claim the boy. Bringing his eyes back down, he offered a smile to try and comfort him. "Are your parents around here?"

He cringed as soon as he said the words. Of course, the boy wouldn't be able to know what he was saying. He needed to get the child back outside and away from here so he could try figuring out what to do with him.

Moving slightly, still holding his jacket, he motioned for him to come with him. But the boy shook his head fiercely, making a small groaning cry as he pulled back against Logan's arm. His eyes had grown so large they filled his small face and tears started to stream back down his cheeks.

He pointed toward the front of the room where Logan had first seen the woman being brought out onto the platform. Logan had forgotten all about whatever was transpiring up there, but his eyes took everything in now.

He could see her better now, and as he watched, she lifted her head and looked across the room with the regal grace of a princess looking at her subjects. Logan's breath caught as her eyes met his. Her eyes were dark, as far as he could tell from where he stood. There was a bruise that extended from the top of her cheekbone, up and around one eye. Her sad gaze softened when she looked at the boy beside him. He could see her lips tighten into a smile as she gave a slight nod to the child.

The boy tried to pull and get away from Logan then, moving to get to the platform. He was making painful noises that made Logan's heart ache at the sorrow he could hear. Whoever this woman was, she was important to this boy.

Holding him tight, Logan moved slightly closer too, wanting to get a better look. *What was going on?* The skin on the back of his neck prickled as he fought against the direction his thoughts were taking him. As soon as he saw the large man stand up beside her, pushing her in front of him, he had a sinking suspicion he was right.

His eyes slowly moved down the front of her torn dress, and locked on the chains that were wrapped around her ankles.

The man's loud voice boomed out, getting the crowd into a fury as he spoke the opening bid.

They were auctioning this poor girl off to the highest bidder. And, bringing his eyes back up, he drew his breath in when he met her stare. The way she stood, resigned to her fate without any hope of getting away from the situation beyond her control, destroyed any chance he had of walking away.

He wasn't sure how he'd do it, but he knew he wasn't leaving her here to face what these men had in mind for her.

CHAPTER 4

*H*ope tried not to let her eyes fall back to her brother. She'd seen him standing there, and her heart had broken knowing he was watching. And she had no way to make sure he got away safely. If Sadie saw him, he'd pay for running away last night.

She'd never felt so completely hopeless in her entire life. Vaguely, she heard the words being spoken, and men shouting back with their bids. The room around her spun and her legs started to tremble as she fought to stand with her head held high. She might be about to lose her freedom, and end up facing who knows what by the end of this auction, but she wasn't going to let them take her dignity.

And she had no intentions of going quietly or

without a fight. She just wished Max had listened to her and stayed safely at Camille's. Now she had him to worry about too.

One man's voice suddenly became louder as he repeatedly countered everyone else's bids. Her head slowly turned and she realized he was the man standing by Max. He had his hand on her brother's shoulder, and his eyes never wavered from hers. Even when he shouted back in response to the bidding—he watched her—his blue eyes the only bright spot in the darkness of the room.

The bidding was slowing down as the price got higher. There weren't as many men taking part any more, but they all watched with interest as the final few continued to fight to win her.

"Come on, men! You've got yourself the use of this fine young lady to tend to your house and any other duties you see fit. You can see for yourselves she's a feisty one who'll be able to take care of all your needs."

Bile rose in her throat at the way the man spoke. She couldn't believe these men all seriously thought they'd just be able to keep her. The only way they'd manage that was if they chained her in a room somewhere. Because as soon as she found a chance, she was getting away.

Finally, it was down to just two men. One was a large man with a moustache that curled out to the sides. His hair was slicked back and he wore a long duster. As the bidding went higher, his skin kept going redder as he turned to glare at the other man.

The other man, however, calmly kept his eyes on hers. He'd immediately accept the next bid, never wavering as his opponent fought against his rising anger. The men around them were all now watching with growing excitement, probably unable to believe how high the bidding was going.

She held her breath as silence filled the air, waiting as no more bids were shouted. The man by her brother slowly turned to look at the other, waiting to see if he would counter the last amount.

"You can have her. She ain't worth that much."

The larger man turned and stormed away, and the man beside her shouted, "Sold!"

She was pushed harshly from behind, and she fell to her knees, unable to hold her balance with her hands and feet tied. The room around her exploded with cheering, and men patted the winning bidder on his back as he made his way to the platform.

He strode toward her, still holding onto her

brother's collar. Max was moving just as fast, and when he got to her, he crouched down and wrapped his small arms around her neck.

How she wished she could hug him back. She couldn't even sign to let him know she was all right, or to tell him to run and get to Camille's like she'd told him to do in the first place.

"Untie her. Now."

The man's voice shook with anger as he glared at the unkempt man who'd been doing the auction.

"Take it easy, mister. As soon as you're all paid up, you're free to take her and untie her. Until we have the money, she still belongs to us."

Hope lifted her head and watched as the man with the blue eyes threw some bills at the one who'd been doing the auction. Once the money had been counted twice to make sure it was all there, she was yanked back up to her feet. Before she knew what was happening, the man who'd bought her reached out and grabbed the other's arm and twisted it sharply.

"You've got your money, so she's mine now. And I don't care much for seeing a woman being treated harshly. So, I'm going to ask you again nicely—untie her."

The men stared each other down, until finally

the one who'd been rough with her pulled his arm free and bent over to untie her arms. Finally feeling the scratchy rope fall away, she rubbed the skin on her wrists to soothe the burning.

He then crouched down, working with a key to unlock the chains wrapped around her legs. Sadie had followed through on her promise to make sure she wasn't going to get away, shackling Hope in chains before they left the house this morning.

But before she could enjoy the freedom of the chains falling to the ground, she spotted Sadie coming from a side door. The woman's face was beaming with happiness at the windfall she'd just received from the auction. Hope desperately wanted to slap the smirk off the woman's face, but she needed to warn Max and get him away.

Moving her hands quickly, she told him to get to Camille's and stay there until she could come for him.

"Grab that boy! He's mine, and he ran off last night, the ungrateful brat."

She was too late. Sadie's voice ripped through the room, and Hope could see the fear in Max's eyes as he fought against staying with her or running like Hope was telling him to do.

Finally, he turned to run, quickly darting past

the people who were trying to grab him and out through the door at the back. Her chains finally fell to the ground, and the man who'd paid for her grabbed her arm to pull her away from the commotion that was breaking out around them. He never slowed down, dragging her behind him amid the shouting of the men, and Sadie who could still be heard screaming for someone to catch Max.

They went out the side door and as soon as they were outside, he stopped and looked around before pulling her across the street and away from the back alley tavern. He turned to look at her and somehow she sensed that she wasn't in any danger from him.

"Who is that boy, and why are they after him?"

"His name is Max. He's my brother. That woman you saw in there was our stepmother, and she's decided Max needs to be sent to an orphanage to punish me for trying to get away from her." Her eyes searched around them, hoping for a sign that Max had managed to get away. He'd gone out the back door, so she had no way of knowing.

"We need to get to him before she does. Please!"

She didn't know why she was asking this man

for help—a man who'd come to an auction to buy himself a woman wasn't the sort she thought could be trusted. But at the moment, she didn't have any other options.

They stood for a moment on the street, dust swirling around them as horses rode past. People were milling around, carrying on with their business completely unaware of the illegal auction that had just taken place in one of the buildings they walked past.

Although she had to admit that by the looks of the people in this area of the city, she didn't think they'd care either way.

"Where would he go?"

She breathed a sigh of relief as she realized he was going to help her. Even though he was a stranger, and she likely should be trying to get away from him now while she could, something told her to take the help he was willing to give.

She figured at this point, she had nothing else to lose.

CHAPTER 5

*H*e was fairly certain he'd completely lost his mind. Chasing after a pick-pocket into the seediest end of Sacramento hadn't been his biggest mistake today. Now, here he was racing to find a young deaf boy, the same one who'd stolen from him, before someone else found him.

Logan had been in some strange situations in his life, but none that would compare with the past hour.

"So, do you mind telling me your name? I figure since I just spent close to a life's savings to get you out of that place, I should at least be able to call you by name." He was trying to ease some of the tension and fear he could see on her face as they hurried along the streets. She seemed to know where she was going, every now and then stopping at a corner and looking around to make sure she knew where she was, before hurrying off again.

He had no choice but to follow and try his best to keep up.

If he had any sense at all, he'd be headed back to the wagon and James where he'd left them. Other than the fact he'd just spent Ella's entire sum of money she'd given him to pick up her mare, he didn't have any reason to feel like he needed to stay with this girl. And honestly, what kind of man risks his own neck to save a kid who stole from him no more than an hour ago?

She looked over at him with a scowl as she moved along the street, holding her skirts in front of her to avoid stepping on them. "My name's Hope Saunders. And the boy you were with is my brother, Max." She slowed slightly and tilted her head to the side. "Why were you with my brother anyway?"

"Well, your brother took it upon himself to steal my wallet. I was merely catching up with him to reclaim my property. He led me to where you were."

"Oh, poor Max. He must have been so scared."

Logan's eyebrow lifted and he almost tripped

over his own feet as he tried to keep up. "Poor Max? Maybe the boy should have been taught right from wrong, including stealing."

Hope stopped and turned to glare at him. "Max does know right from wrong. Unfortunately, things haven't been easy for him the past few months, and seeing his sister put up for auction while he's left wondering where he'll end up may have caused him to make some bad decisions. It's obvious he was going to try using the money to buy my freedom. He's a good kid, and quite frankly, coming from a man who just spent his life savings on a woman, I'd say you're hardly in any position to criticize Max."

She whirled back around, lifting her skirts once more as she lifted her chin and stomped away. His chin dropped and he stood unsure if he should take this opportunity to just get as far away from this situation as he could, or if he should continue to try helping the woman who was obviously ungrateful.

Catching back up to her, he reached out and held her arm, stopping her. "Hold on just a minute. I just finished saving you from being bought by only God knows what kind of man, and you have the nerve to accuse me of being no better than them? If you remember, I just finished telling you I had chased your brother there to get my wallet back, nothing more. In fact, I was planning to get as far away from there as I could once I had my money, but then I saw a sad-looking, brown-haired girl who looked like she could use some help. I have no intentions of keeping you, and in fact, you're more than free to go now. But a thank-you might be nice. Especially since the money I spent to save you wasn't really mine to spend."

He watched the muscles in her jaw clench and her throat move as she swallowed. "I'm sorry. I haven't had the luxury of having anyone I could trust for a very long time, and at the moment, I need to find my brother. My stepmother is a vindictive woman who will send him as far away from me as she can, especially if she realizes I'm not going to be suffering as much as she'd hoped."

Logan started walking again, so she fell into step beside him. "In case you were wondering, my name is Logan Wallace." He twisted his head to look at her, noticing how the sunlight reflected off the shine of her hair. "Let's find your brother."

∼

HOPE FOUGHT against the panic that was starting to rise. She paced back and forth in front of the open doorway where they were standing on the front porch. "Are you sure, Camille? He never came here at all?"

"I'm sorry, Hope. I had no idea any of this was going on. He never came last night and he hasn't been here today." Her friend turned to go back inside. "Just give me a moment to grab my coat and I'll come help you search."

"No, Camille. I can't get you involved. You can't afford to lose your position as governess in this house. I shouldn't have even told Max to come here in the first place. If you'd been caught, I know Sadie would have turned the blame onto you."

Camille reached out and took Hope's hands in hers. Hope could see the tears in her friend's eyes. "So what will happen to you now? Where will you go?"

Pulling her friend in for a quick hug, Hope tried to reassure herself as much as her friend. "We'll be fine. I have to find Max before Sadie does. As soon as I can, I'll send you a message to let you know where we are."

When she pulled away, she looked to Logan who was waiting for her to finish talking to

Camille. He'd stood quietly as they said their goodbyes.

"I think I know where he might be."

He pushed himself off the railing where he'd been leaning and started to walk down the steps. She quickly ran to keep up with him, not having the chance to say anything else to her friend as they started up the street again.

"Where? How could you possibly know where my brother would be? I thought you said you weren't from around here."

"I'm not, but I do know if I was a scared young boy and the only person I had in the world was my sister, I'd be headed in the direction of where I knew she was going."

She struggled to keep up with him, lifting her heavy skirts as she tried to make her steps match his. "But how could he possibly know where I'd be going?"

By now, they were back into the familiar area of Sacramento. She instinctively reached her hand up to try patting her hair into some semblance of order, not wanting the people she knew to see her so disheveled.

She rolled her eyes at herself as she realized

that was the last thing she should be worrying about at the moment.

Logan quickly strode across the street, headed toward a wagon that was parked in front of one of the stores. He went straight over and pulled back the canvas and peeked behind some of the boxes.

"Logan! Where did you end up?" An older man came from up the street, moving as fast as his legs would take him. "Did you get your wallet back?"

"Yes, I did." Logan wasn't looking at the man. He continued to pull sheets back and move boxes around in the back of the wagon.

The older man was looking at her, obviously unsure why she was standing on the street while Logan was now jumping up into the wagon and rummaging through the supplies. She put her hand out to let him take hers. "My name is Hope. Logan is helping me find my brother."

"I'm James O'Hara, ma'am. I'll admit to being just a slight bit confused as to what's going on here."

"I knew it." Logan ripped back a sheet near the front of the wagon. Hope sobbed as she saw the tear-stained face staring back at her. When her brother started to stand up, Logan placed his hand on the boy's shoulder and pushed him back down with a shake of the head.

"Tell him to stay here. If he stands up, someone might see him."

Hope ran to the back of the wagon, desperately wanting to climb in and comfort her brother. She signed and told Max to sit still and stay where he was.

"We are going to get in the wagon and drive out of town to where my men are waiting with the cattle. You can have the chance to talk to him then."

Hope told Max what Logan was telling her, hoping the young boy could understand.

"Logan, you were supposed to meet with the buyer for Ella's horse at noon. We can't just leave town now."

Logan threw the blanket back over Max, then hopped down from the wagon and thrust his hands through his hair. "We have to leave town, James. I don't have the money for Ella's horse anyway."

"What do you mean you don't have the money? I thought you said you got the wallet back."

"Oh, I got the wallet back. But I had to spend the money on something else."

The older man was following Logan around to the seat of the wagon. It was clear the man was confused and getting frustrated that he wasn't getting any answers. Hope had no choice but to follow them around to the front.

"What could you possibly have spent that much money on in the amount of time you were gone?"

Logan grinned and nodded his head in her direction. "You're looking at her."

CHAPTER 6

"That poor boy must be exhausted. I can't even imagine what he's been through." James was looking over by the wagon where Hope crouched down tucking blankets around Max. The darkness of the night was broken only by the light from the flickering fire where they were sitting.

"Do you think they'll come out here looking for him?" Luke was leaning back against a log, resting an arm on his turned up knee.

Logan watched as Hope sat down on the ground next to her brother, leaning over to rub the hair from his eyes.

"I have no idea. Honestly, I've never been in the middle of anything so confusing. All I know is, Hope has told me her stepmother needed money so put her up for auction. When Hope and Max tried to run away last night before it happened, she caught Hope and forced her to stay. Max got away, but no one knows for sure where he even stayed last night." Hope was now bent down, hugging her brother.

"I swear, when I saw her standing up there with all those men hanging around ready to bid on her, I thought I was going to be sick. What kind of person can do that to someone else? So, I'd say if her stepmother was capable of doing that, I have no doubt she'd try to find Max just to be spiteful. If she finds out who bought Hope, she might come looking."

Luke shook his head. "Well, we'll be on the trail first thing in the morning. I've told the men to be ready. The sooner we can get them away from here, the better."

They sat in silence, listening to the sound of the cattle moving around on the other side of the wagon, and the other night wildlife that was just starting to make their way into the darkness.

"I'm going to turn in. It's going to be a long trip home for these old bones." James stood up and stretched. "You did the right thing, Logan. I know Ella will understand."

The man nodded at him as he patted him on the shoulder on his way past. He headed to the bedrolls that were laid out on the other side of the fire.

Luke stood up too. "I'm going to check on the cattle one more time. I just want to make sure everyone is keeping watch." Logan watched him walk over to the herd he could faintly see in the distance.

Logan knew he should be the one worrying about the condition of his cows and the men in his charge. Instead, he sat by the fire trying to make sense out of everything that had happened in the past twelve hours.

He was so lost in his thoughts, staring into the moving flames that he jumped when Hope walked into view.

"I'm sorry. I didn't mean to disturb you." She stood just to the side, holding her hands in front of her. The light from the fire highlighted the dark purple bruise around her eye, making Logan's stomach clench with anger.

She came closer and turned to look down into the fire without moving for the longest time. The crackling of the logs seemed to have hypnotized her.

"It's not much, but you can have a seat on this crate." He motioned to the overturned box James had been sitting on. She turned and looked at it before moving to sit. As she did, she smoothed out her skirt, which was badly torn in quite a few places.

"I haven't had the chance to thank you for saving me today. I'm not really sure if there's any way I could ever repay you."

Logan shrugged, not feeling comfortable being praised. "I couldn't just leave you there."

Her head turned slowly, and her eyes locked on his. "Yes, you could have. You didn't know me, and it would have been easy enough to turn and walk out. But you didn't."

He could see her chin tremble slightly. "And then you helped me find Max."

He looked back to the fire. "You're free to go, you know. Once I get you far enough away from your stepmother, you and your brother can leave. I don't want you thinking just because I paid for you, that I honestly believe you belong to me or anything."

He cringed at his lame attempt at letting her know he wasn't planning on actually making her stay because he'd paid for her.

"No, I don't think that. But I'm not leaving. I have a debt to you, and I intend to pay it."

His head whipped back to look at her. "What do you mean?" Surely she didn't think he was like those other men in the tavern.

"I know how much you paid to get me away from those other men. And I also know that it was money you were supposed to use to buy a horse for your sister. I don't have any money to pay you back, but I can help on the way to Oregon and then once we get there, I will find a way to pay you back."

He shook his head. "Hope, you don't need to pay me back. My sister, Ella, and her husband, Titus, are understanding people. Trust me, they would've been angry if I hadn't used their money to save someone if I could."

She brought her arms up and hugged herself as she leaned into the fire for warmth. "My mother raised me to honor my debts. If someone does something kind for me, then I'm not to let it pass without repaying it in full. And that's what I intend to do."

He was tired and didn't feel like arguing. Somehow he could sense she wasn't the type of woman to back down when she'd made up her mind. He'd wait until they got to the next town and he'd convince her it was best if she stayed there until she could get in contact with some family or friends who could help them.

Suddenly, a thought hit him. "Do you have any other family you can go to?"

She just sat quietly, staring into the fire. Finally, she slowly shook her head. "The only one I have is Max." She said the words so quietly he almost didn't hear her.

She had nowhere else to go.

He couldn't just leave her in a strange town, especially knowing there were likely people looking for them. What odds did a beautiful young woman have alone, with a young deaf child to care for?

Pushing his hand through his hair, he clenched his jaw tight. Now, not only did he have a herd of cattle to take back to Oregon, he had to figure out what to do with Hope and Max. He had no idea how she thought she could possibly help out on the trail. A woman wasn't going to like the dust that was going to be kicked up as they went along, and she sure wasn't going to be happy about how slow they were going to have to move.

And as much as he thought Max was a good

kid, he didn't want to worry about the boy being hurt by a stampede or anything else that he couldn't hear.

When she turned to look at him, her eyes glistened with unshed tears. "I know you didn't ask to be stuck with two extra people, especially not a woman and a boy who likely won't be able to offer you much help. But there's nothing for us here. I won't ask for anything from you, other than a chance to do what I can to repay you for the kindness you've shown me today."

Logan met her gaze and found himself wondering what she had been like before her stepmother tried to ruin her. He pictured a smiling, happy woman who cared deeply for those around her.

And for some reason, he realized he desperately wanted to give her the chance to be that woman again.

"You know, it's not going to be an easy trip back to Oregon. And, Bethany doesn't have a whole lot to offer for a young woman on her own."

She gave him a sad smile. "After what I've been through today, I'm not afraid of some dust and dirt. I just want to get Max somewhere where we can start over. I'll worry about the rest when we get there." Lifting her shoulders, she looked back into the fire. "Besides, I'm not leaving until we're even."

He sighed loudly as he shook his head. "Well then, you'd better get some sleep. We'll be leaving by sun-up."

Somehow he could tell it was going to be a long trip back to Oregon.

CHAPTER 7

"*J*ust letting you know that one of the men noticed some riders making their way toward our camp. You might want to get the boy hidden."

Hope whipped her head around as she heard Luke talking to Logan. "What are we going to do? What if it's someone looking for him?" She put the cloth down she'd been helping the cook clean the dishes with after their breakfast. Her eyes immediately started to scan the area for Max.

Logan was already moving ahead of her. He walked over to the other side of the camp where James was patiently showing Max how to hitch the horses to the wagon. "James, we need to get the boy hidden away somewhere."

Hope came to a stop right behind Logan,

signing for Max to understand what they were doing. Her heart lurched as she saw the fear in his eyes. She couldn't wait until they were far away from this place and Max could go back to being a young boy with no worries.

The men around her were already in action, moving boxes and canvases in the back of the wagon to create a spot to hide him. She couldn't believe how lucky she'd been to end up with these men who were willing to go to such lengths for complete strangers. They'd only just met Max and her, yet they'd already shown more kindness to her than she'd seen in a long time.

Logan had paid a great deal of money to help her, and now he was risking even more by helping to hide Max.

"We need to get him inside a crate that we can make it look like it's still sealed." Logan was standing in the wagon bed, looking around for something that would work. Luke had ridden out to meet whoever was coming, hoping to stall them and give them a bit more time.

James pointed to one at the front. "Take that and dump the flour in the bush over there. We can nail the lid shut again."

Hope gasped and put her hand on the older

man's arm. "But that's a lot of flour to just throw away. You can't do that. It was for your store back in Oregon."

Logan was already lifting the crate, and jumping down from the wagon to head to the bush. "One thing you'll soon find out about James O'Hara—a bit of flour doesn't matter to him if it means helping someone out. And once he's made his mind up, you'd likely have more luck arguing with a tree anyway."

Hope watched as Logan came back to the wagon with the empty crate and put it back at the front. Hope led Max over to crawl up onto the wagon bed. She told him everything would be fine, he'd just have to stay still inside the crate until they came to get him out. He seemed to trust Logan, so he let the man lead him to the front and help him crawl inside.

James threw a hammer to him and reached out with a handful of nails. Once the crate was sealed back up, Logan quickly threw more crates on top and around it.

He was jumping back to the ground just as Luke rode back into the camp with the men who'd been spotted coming their way. "Logan, we've got a few men here looking for a young boy. They say he's the brother to this woman you bought yesterday." Luke looked at her quickly, making sure she knew to play along.

The man in the lead reached down to take Logan's outstretched hand. "Clarence Harding. I've been hired by a Mrs. Sadie Saunders to find a boy who's in her charge. She believes he'll be with his sister, who is now in your possession."

Hope glared at the man who obviously didn't care about the fact the woman who'd hired him had auctioned off a young girl. He was a rough-looking man, with hard eyes that she could tell had no compassion in them at all. She knew there was no point in trying to appeal to him. All they could do was hope they didn't find Max.

Logan leaned against the wagon, staring up at Clarence. "I don't have a young boy here, and I don't appreciate you interrupting my crew as we're about to head out. So, if you have proof the boy's here, you're welcome to let me know. Otherwise, we'll be on our way."

Clarence shrugged, then threw his leg over the back of the horse and hopped down. "Oh, I don't got no proof. Just my suspicions that the boy's here. And I've got a good payday coming to me if I bring him back."

Hope trembled with anger. Sadie had made it clear they had no money, which was why she was auctioning Hope off. How did she all of a sudden have enough money to hire a thug to find Max? She wouldn't have wasted the money she'd got from the auction to chase after them out of spite.

Logan must have been thinking the same thing as he crinkled his brows together and looked her way.

The three men with Clarence all got down from their horses, resting their hands on the guns at their hips. Obviously, they were ready for a fight if it came down to it.

Luke dismounted and came over to stand by Logan and James.

Her heart pounded as she realized these men could end up hurt because of her. And if something did happen to them, she'd be at the mercy of these thugs.

She clenched her hands tightly in front of her as she fought the trembling of her body. She couldn't let these ruffians see her fear.

Finally, after what seemed like an eternity, Logan stepped to the side and swept his arm around the camp. "You're more than welcome to take a look around. But we're leaving as soon as we get everything ready to go. So you better hurry. We're not sticking around waiting for you to find someone who isn't here."

Logan came toward her, meeting her eyes as he reached out and gently took her arm to turn her away. She walked beside him, not wanting to leave the wagon.

"Logan, we can't walk away. What if they get too close to the crate?" she whispered the words carefully, quickly peeking back to see the men starting to search around the wagon and spreading out to the rest of the camp. Luke and James stood watch.

"That's exactly why I'm bringing you over here. You can't hide your emotions well enough from your face. They'd know instantly they were close to him if you were standing over there."

"What are we going to do if they find him?"

She looked up at his face, watching his jaw muscles clench as he stared ahead. "We'll worry about that if it happens."

They stopped over by the chuckwagon so Logan could fill the cook in on what was happening. No doubt they'd be going through his wagon too. The older man, Frank, looked down at Hope. When she'd offered to help him this morning, he'd been happy to let her put on an apron and step in. He was a gruff man who seemed to say whatever was on his mind, so she automatically cringed as she waited to see what he'd ask.

"Why are they after the boy?"

The only ones who knew the whole story were Logan, James, and Luke. The rest of the men had just been told Hope and Max were making the trip to Oregon with them, and no one had asked any questions.

Hope swallowed and met his gaze. "They want to put him in an orphanage because I'm not of age to be his legal guardian." She didn't think he needed all the details.

He didn't even blink, watching her intently. Finally, he nodded slightly. "Well, an orphanage ain't no place for a young boy, especially not when he has someone who loves him."

With those words, he turned back to finish packing up his wagon as though there wasn't anything out of the ordinary about a group of men searching for a young boy.

"I'm going to go back over and make sure they hurry things up. Stay here and help Frank clean up. We'll be on the trail in under an hour." Logan seemed so sure of the words he spoke, it gave her some confidence he was right.

As she watched him walk back over, she held her breath when a couple of the men moved crates around in the wagon. They were lifting canvases and looking in every corner, between each box and under every lid they could open.

Seeing Logan back over there gave her comfort. She didn't know how, but she just knew he'd keep Max safe.

CHAPTER 8

*H*e stared at the open ground ahead of him, thankful they were finally on their way. The long grass around them swayed slowly with the breeze, while the large birds flew overhead looking for their prey. The day was already warm, and as they made their way along the trail, Logan finally had some time to try making sense out of everything that had happened in the past day.

Turning his head, he could see Hope and Max settled in beside James in the wagon. He was riding to the side, making sure the trail ahead was clear as the cattle and cowboys he'd hired followed behind.

He didn't have a clue what to do with them. He'd come to California to pick up some cattle to start his own herd on the property he'd bought in

Oregon. Plus, Ella's mare. Her husband, Titus, would have made the trip, but figured since Logan was going anyway, he could just pick it up and bring it back.

It was supposed to be an easy, quick trip to pick everything up and head home without incident.

He was pretty sure things couldn't have gone more wrong. He knew both his sister and Titus would understand about the money, so that didn't really worry him. He'd make sure they were paid back somehow.

The thing that had him worried the most was how he was supposed to keep Hope's reputation intact while they made their way home. Not to mention, keep both her and Max safe along the way.

Shaking his head as he groaned to himself, he sunk a bit into the saddle and allowed a few moments of feeling sorry for himself. He was still just a young man himself, and to be honest, he'd never had to take on a responsibility like this before.

But when those men had come looking for Max, something had reared up inside him like he'd never felt before. He'd been prepared to do whatever it took to protect that boy, and it didn't make any sense to him. As they'd searched around the wagon and the camp, Logan had been ready for a fight if it had come to that.

Thankfully, the men had left, but Logan knew in his gut that wasn't likely the last they were going to hear from Sadie or those hired thugs.

His eyes found their way back around to the wagon bouncing along the trail. Hope sat with her arm around her brother, laughing at something James was telling them. He was grateful the older man had been with him so he could help take on some of the burden of caring for them.

Logan wondered how with everything Hope had been through over the past few days, she could sit and laugh about anything. He knew they literally had nothing with them but the clothes on their backs, having to flee from Sacramento without returning home for any of their possessions.

And the bruising still evident on her face indicated exactly what kind of treatment she'd endured before he found her at that auction.

Yet there she sat, smiling and talking with James like she didn't have a care in the world. She'd sign to her brother when James would say something, and Max would smile. However, Logan could see the boy was having a harder time coming to terms with everything that had happened. His smile wasn't as real as Hope's. Max had faced so much while dealing with his own burdens, and it made Logan angry to think of the fear the child had lived through.

Logan wasn't much older than Max was now when they'd come out west to make a new life in Oregon. Along the way, his father had died, and it had taken Logan a long time to get over the pain of what had happened.

Clicking his heels into his horse's sides, he rode over to the wagon and pulled up alongside James. Hope smiled over at him, while Max looked at him warily.

They'd waited until they were well down the trail and the riders had gone back in the other direction and out of sight before they'd stopped to let Max out of the crate. He'd been upset and scared when they'd finally opened the lid, and Logan suspected he might even blame him a bit for having to stay inside for so long.

It was difficult to make a child understand when something was being done in their best interests.

"It's a good day to put Sacramento behind us. Nothing but clear skies as far as the eye can see."

James grinned widely as he turned his head to take in the view ahead of them.

Logan nodded his head toward Max. "How's the boy doing?"

James smiled down at the child. "He seems all right now that he's been able to get out and ride up front with us."

"Yes, Mr. Wallace, Max is doing much better. I'm not sure he's enjoying bumping along in the wagon, but he'll get used to it." Hope smiled up at him from the other side of the wagon bench.

His eyebrow went up as she finished talking. "Mr. Wallace? Why are you calling me that?"

He couldn't be sure, but he almost thought Hope rolled her eyes slightly. "Because where I come from, calling a man who isn't well known to the family by their given name would be considered improper. Just because I may have had a lapse in my manners during the first day we met, doesn't mean I won't be more careful now that I've had a chance for my nerves to settle a bit."

Logan's mouth hung open as he watched Hope press at her skirts, as though she might be able to remove some of the wrinkles that were evident. He wasn't sure what she planned to do with the rips and the dirt stains from the hem. He laughed out loud before he could stop himself.

The absurdity of her trying to be "proper" while sitting in her one tattered dress, her hair in a mess of knots from not even having a brush to attend to it, struck him as immensely funny. And she was going to call him Mr. Wallace.

He'd never been called Mr. Wallace in his life, and he certainly wasn't about to let it happen now.

But before he could correct her, her eyes pulled together and she glared at him. Surely this was some kind of joke. Maybe James had thought it would be funny to convince her to say all that.

However, the look on her face soon erased that thought.

"Hope, I appreciate the fact that you may have been brought up to use the more formal way to address a man, but I assure you right now, if you call me Mr. Wallace, I won't be inclined to answer. So if you want me to reply, I'd suggest you continue to call me Logan."

Her mouth opened to answer, and he could tell already she was going to argue. But after the morning he'd had, he really wasn't in the mood. He put his hand up to stop her from speaking. "I came over to see if Max would like to get a break from the wagon's bouncing and come for a ride up ahead to see where we can make camp for the night."

"No, he won't want to do that. He's very timid." Hope shook her head for emphasis.

Logan leaned forward in the saddle. Max was looking back and forth between them as they spoke, obviously picking up on the tension. He smiled at the boy and motioned with his head down toward his horse. He pointed to Max, then down at the saddle.

"Could you please ask him for me? Let him decide." Logan had seen the way his eyes lit up as he started to understand what Logan was asking him.

Hope was obviously wrestling with her need to be polite and do as Logan was asking, and wanting to keep her brother safe on the seat beside her. Logan knew she'd had to step up and protect her brother a lot in the past few days, and likely even long before that.

But it wasn't fair to Max to be held back from doing something that might be fun for him. Finally, Hope moved her hands and asked Max if he'd like to ride with Logan. The boy's smile spread across his face instantly, and he looked up at Logan like he'd hung the sun in the sky.

James stopped the wagon, and took Max's hand to help him get across and over to the horse. Logan took his hand, and helped him climb up in front of him. Even though Max was ten, he had a small frame, and Logan thought he'd be safer in the front until he'd been on a horse a bit more. Growing up in the city, he likely hadn't had much opportunity to ride horseback.

"Don't go too fast. Max hasn't ridden a horse before. He's still small, so you make sure you hang on to him." Hope was moving her hands quickly, saying something to Max, who nodded.

Logan tapped the boy on the shoulder to get him to look back at him. He motioned with his lips and hands to ask if he was ready. Max's smile lit up his whole face as he nodded quickly.

Reaching up to tip his hat down slightly in Hope's direction, he raised his eyebrows and slowly urged the horse forward while she was left standing in the wagon, wringing her hands in front of her.

They went a few paces ahead of the wagon so Max could get a feel for the motion of the horse.

But once they'd gone a ways out, he put his arm tighter around the boy and kicked in his heels.

His horse took off, and leaning forward slightly to look down at Max, Logan saw the pure joy on his face. It made it all worthwhile.

Even at the cost of knowing he was going to be in trouble with Max's sister, who was already loudly yelling at him from her perch in the wagon behind them.

CHAPTER 9

*H*ope pulled her fingers through her hair, doing her best to get some of the tangles out. She knew it must look a fright, and since she hadn't even been able to grab a bonnet, it was full of knots. Finally getting the worst of it smoothed out, she put a loose braid in and tied the end with some string.

Her body ached from bouncing in the wagon for the past week, not to mention sleeping on the ground. She slept tucked up close to Max under James O'Hara's wagon at night, while the men slept around the fire. Logan had rigged up some pieces of canvas to hang from the sides to give them some privacy and warmth. There was always a man taking turns standing guard on the other side of the wagon throughout the night.

Whenever she thought about the way this group of men had taken them in and offered their protection, she'd get a lump in her throat. And ever since the day he'd ridden with Logan on the horse, it seemed as though Max was finally back to his happy self before all of this started.

He had the smile back on his face, and he followed Logan everywhere he went. The strange part was, Hope had noticed Logan really didn't seem to mind. He was so patient with Max, working to understand whatever he was saying. And she'd also noticed James, Luke, and even gruff old Frank taking the time to try communicating however they could with Max.

It warmed her heart, even when the worries would start poking in to her mind about what would happen once they'd arrived in Oregon. She wanted to pay Logan back somehow, not just for the money he'd spent to save her, but for allowing them to come with them. She knew he didn't have to do that and could have insisted on leaving them in Sacramento.

But what would they do once she'd paid him back? They had no family, and there weren't many openings for young women on their own to be able to earn money to support themselves. Logan had said Bethany didn't have many opportunities, so they might have to continue on their way to Oregon City.

Knowing she couldn't fall asleep yet, she carefully pulled the canvas back and quietly crawled out from under the wagon. The night air was cool, but she welcomed it on her skin that had already seen more sun in the past week than it had in her lifetime.

As she came out into the light of the fire, the man standing watch nodded and smiled at her. She walked over toward the fire, careful not to wake any of the men who were on their bedrolls on the other side.

Folding her legs under her, she sat on the ground and looked up at the sky. Stars lit up the darkness as far as her eyes could see. Far away in the distance, a wolf sent its cry up into the stillness of the night. Everything was so unfamiliar to her. Growing up in the comfort of the city, in a home filled with light, she'd never had the chance to notice how calm and enchanting the night could be.

"It's beautiful, isn't it?"

Logan's voice startled her, and she quickly turned her head to look at him as he sat down beside her. He stretched his legs out, almost touching the fire with his boots, and leaned back on his arms. His attention was on the sky and she didn't think he'd even realized he'd scared her.

She looked back up, pulling her knees in close and hugging them with her arms. "Yes, it is. I'd never really noticed before."

"You wouldn't notice it in the city. It's one of the first things I miss when I have to go away from home, and why I could never live in a city."

Turning her head slightly, she peeked at Logan. His dark hair was a little too long, and the front was hanging down onto his forehead. He wasn't wearing the hat that was normally pulled down, shielding his eyes from the sun. Even in the darkness, the firelight showed the bright blue of his eyes gazing up at the stars.

She remembered the first time she'd seen those blue eyes staring at her in that room. She hadn't even realized it then, but when she thought back now, she'd sensed the strength and kindness behind them.

"Have you always lived in Oregon?"

She realized she'd never really asked him much about his life over the past week they'd been on the trail.

He continued to look up at the sky, and she wondered if he was even going to answer.

"No, we came out west when I was just a boy. I was about twelve or thirteen when we set out along the Oregon Trail for a better life out west. My father had paid for a claim in a new settlement just inside the Willamette Valley, and he was excited to have a new start."

She waited for him to continue, watching the expressions moving across his face.

"But he drowned while we were crossing the Snake River. He jumped in to save my older brother Colton and was pulled along by the current. When we got to Bethany, we set about making our new home without him."

His throat moved as he swallowed. "My oldest brother, Reid was only sixteen, and Colton and Ella were fifteen. So, we all had to grow up fast and do what our father had intended to do."

She sensed sadness in him as he spoke about his father, even after all this time. But she could understand it well.

"Is your mom still in Bethany?"

A smile spread across his face. "Yes, my ma is just about the strongest lady I know. Well, maybe my sister Ella. I don't think I'd want to get into a fight with her."

"It must be wonderful to have such a large family." She'd always envied people with big families.

He shrugged. "I suppose. It can be hard though too. There was a time not too long ago when my older brothers got into a fight over a woman. Colton left for a long time, leaving me to take over his work. My youngest brother, Connor, was still just a boy, so I had to work alongside Reid to keep the farm going."

"Have they worked things out now?" She was trying to remember all the names he'd mentioned, while imagining what they'd look like.

He finally turned and looked at her. Rolling his eyes, he laughed quietly. "They've both fallen in love and aren't anywhere near as grumpy and unbearable now as they were growing up. It's funny what a woman can do to a man."

He was shaking his head as he laughed at the fate of his brothers. Raising her eyebrow, she pinned her gaze on his. "And exactly what is it that a woman does?"

His eyes flickered briefly with what looked like panic as he realized what he'd just said. "Well, just that now they're a little softer than they used to be."

Quickly changing the subject, he kept his eyes on hers. "How about your family? How did you end up in the clutches of that horrible woman?"

Sighing loudly, she turned to look at the fire. "After my mother died a few years ago, my father was having a hard time figuring out how to look after a young daughter and a son who was deaf. It was my mom who took time to learn to sign language in order to teach Max. My father never wanted to. He'd been devastated at having a less than perfect son. And he married Sadie to give us someone to replace our mother."

Logan let out a low whistle beside her, and she turned to see him looking at her with his eyebrows pulled firmly together. "How in the world did your father think a woman like her would be suitable to look after two children? I'd rather ask the devil himself to pay a visit at my house."

A small laugh escaped before she could stop herself, and she quickly covered her mouth with her hand. With her eyes wide, she shook her head before letting her hand down to reply. "While that may be true, I'm sure my father had his reasons. He was missing my mother terribly, so perhaps he just wanted someone to help him, and in his grief, he couldn't see Sadie for who she truly was."

"Well, I'd imagine he had to see it after he married her."

Hope looked into the flames again. "By then, he was so far gone with drinking and spending his days and nights at the tavern, I don't think he cared anymore." An ache in her stomach made her pull her legs in tighter and she rested her chin on her knees. "I tried to protect Max from the worst of it, but Sadie always threatened to send him away if I said anything. Then when my father died, she had control of everything. I don't know if I can rightfully have custody of Max even when I do turn eighteen in couple of weeks. Sadie says Max was left in her care."

All the worries she'd been having pushed their way in again. "I'm going to have to hide from her and make sure she never finds us. I think eventually she'll give up, because she has nothing to gain from having us around anyway. I'm sure she's just after Max to make me suffer."

Logan sat up and shook his head. "I don't know. It seems like she's pretty intent on finding him."

He quickly looked at her and his eyes widened when she gasped slightly. "But don't worry. We'll do everything we can to keep you safe. We won't let her find you." He'd obviously realized he hadn't thought his words out carefully.

Swallowing against the worry building inside her, she kept her eyes on his.

"But what will happen when we get to Oregon, and we don't have your protection anymore?" The words tumbled out of her mouth in a quiet whisper.

His eyes never moved from hers. "I give you my word, she won't hurt you."

As she heard him speak, she had no doubt he meant every word.

CHAPTER 10

"**I** reckon you're going to have a happy woman when she sees what you've got here. You're a good man, Logan, and I have no doubt, Hope will see it too."

"Well, I'm not doing it to impress her. I'm just being practical. She needed something to wear. That dress is just about ready to fall off her."

James slapped him on the shoulder. "I still feel bad. I can't believe I overlooked basic necessities for a woman when I was stocking up to bring things back to Oregon. I'm sure Mrs. O'Hara is going to have plenty to say when she finds out."

Logan laughed as he imagined Susan O'Hara scolding her husband for not bringing any fancy combs, brushes or other lady items back to their store. James had been practical, picking up items that cost him more to have shipped up to Bethany, but hadn't thought of some of the finer things he could have brought back.

When Logan had asked James if he had a brush or a dress Hope could have until they got home, the older man had been so disappointed in himself for not having anything. He had many bolts of fabric, but no completed dresses. And since there weren't many women around Bethany, he hadn't even thought of something as simple as a brush.

So Logan had been up before the sun and ridden into the small town just west of where they'd stopped for the night and managed to find two sturdy skirts and a couple of blouses. They weren't anything fancy, but it was all they'd had in the only mercantile in town. He'd guessed at her size, but the waist could be pulled tighter if she needed to. In truth, he was a bit nervous to even give them to her. Even though the dress she wore now was ripped and dirty, it was still obvious it was of a high quality. Hope had come from a different background, and most likely wouldn't have ever had to wear a serviceable skirt for life on the frontier.

The brush and comb set he'd managed to get wasn't made of high quality materials either. He was sure she'd be used to having something much fancier, but he hoped these would do until she could get something better.

Heat rose in his cheeks as he remembered the man in the store asking him if he also needed some "unmentionables" for his lady. Logan hadn't even thought about those, but had quickly declined, not prepared to face the embarrassment of having to hand anything like that over to Hope.

"Mr. Wallace, were you able to pick up all the supplies you had to run into town for?" Hope's voice startled him from behind, and he whipped around quickly to face her.

Sighing loudly, he pushed his hat back slightly and shook his head. "Hope, I've told you so many times, my name is Logan. I swear, if you don't start calling me by my given name, I'm not going to give you the surprise I picked up while I was in town."

They had been on the trail now for well over a week, and she still insisted on calling him Mr. Wallace. He almost got the impression she just did it to annoy him. She knew how much he hated it.

He'd had the storekeeper wrap the clothing and brush set in some brown paper to keep them from getting dusty before he even got back to the camp.

She tipped her head slightly and looked at him

warily. "What did you get me? I already owe you so much, I can't imagine why you'd do more to add to my debt to you."

Clenching his jaw, he groaned. "And I've told you that you don't owe me anything. Why do you insist on arguing with me about this?" Every day, at least once, she mentioned the money he'd paid, and the care he'd provided her and Max with ever since.

Pulling the package from behind his back, he handed it to her. Max came running over from finishing helping James get the horses hitched. He pointed at the package and moved his hands to speak to Hope.

"What's he saying?" Logan was starting to pick up some of the basic signs, but still couldn't understand most of it.

"He just told me to hurry up and open it. He wants to see what you got me."

Logan smiled at the boy. Max was waiting patiently to see what was inside the paper. Most kids would be upset that they hadn't got anything, but he was standing there grinning at his sister like it was Christmas.

Reaching into his pocket, he pulled out a candy stick he'd also picked up for Max and held it out in front of him. Max's eyes lit up, and he stared up at Logan as though he was handing him a pony.

Logan pointed to Max, and mouthed the words, "For you."

Max took it and held it in front of him, looking down at it as though he were holding a gold bar in his hands. Suddenly, the boy flung himself at Logan, almost knocking him off balance as his small arms went around his waist.

Looking down at the top of the boy's head, Logan's heart lurched. Max was so thankful for anything, and something as simple as a stick of candy meant so much to him. He brought his hand up and ruffled the child's hair slightly as Max pulled back and looked up at him sheepishly. Logan could tell he was embarrassed at his show of emotion.

Winking at Max, Logan pushed his chin toward Hope. Max turned and stood beside Logan, waiting for her to open her package. She stood completely still, her eyes shining with wetness as she watched Max's reaction to the candy.

"We're waiting, Hope. Max would like to see what you've got in there."

Her hands shook as she looked down at the brown paper and started to untie the string holding it together. As the paper fell away, he suddenly felt uncomfortable, unsure how she'd react.

What if she hated the boring brown skirt made from the thicker material that could withstand life out here?

But as she pulled the first skirt out and opened it up, draping it over her arm, a tear spilled over before she could wipe it away. She ran her fingers over the fabric without saying anything. When she pulled the first cream colored blouse out, she caressed the lighter fabric between her fingers.

She set the items on the back of the chuck-wagon table that was still folded out and took the other pieces out. When she got to the bottom, she gave a cry and brought her hands up to her mouth as she finally looked up at him. Sensing his sister was in distress, Max immediately went over and stood beside her, lifting his head to look at her. He moved his hands, asking her something.

She smiled down and nodded. Moving her mouth and whispering out loud as she signed, she answered him. "I'm fine. Just surprised."

Reaching into the paper, she pulled the brush, comb, and mirror out, hugging them to her chest.

When her gaze met his, his breath caught in his throat.

"Mr...I mean, Logan, you didn't have to do this." Her voice shook with emotion. He was feeling uncomfortable as he tried to act like it wasn't a big deal. But by the happiness he could see on her face, he knew it was to her.

"They aren't as fancy as what you're used to, but I thought you might like to have something a bit more comfortable and suited to being out here on the trail."

Her throat moved as she swallowed. "They're all perfect."

Suddenly, a rumbling sound could be heard and Logan whipped his head around. The dust cloud rising in the air left him with no doubt about what was happening. Something had spooked the cattle and they were running straight toward the camp.

"Stampede!"

CHAPTER 11

*H*ope stood rooted to the spot, watching as the men in the camp all scattered. Logan grabbed her arm and yelled down at her above the thundering noise that was picking up around them. "Can you ride a horse?"

She shook her head, fear rising in her throat as she realized how vulnerable she was. Logan swore loudly before thrusting his hand through his hair. "Stay here. Don't move. We'll do our best to get them under control and hopefully they won't get into the camp."

Holding Max, she pressed his head into her stomach, softly rubbing his hair. But he pushed back, signing to ask what was happening.

"It's a stampede. We have to stay here until Logan and the men can get things under control."

Max's eyes went wide and he turned his head to watch Logan leap onto his horse and ride away. The ground thundered under their feet, so Hope knew Max could sense the danger that was coming their way.

Clouds of dust were already starting to settle around the camp, and Hope looked around for somewhere safe they could stay out of the way. Setting her new brush down, she decided they should climb up onto the back of the chuckwagon so they could at least see if the cattle were getting closer.

Turning to sign to Max to climb up after her, she gasped when she realized he wasn't standing there anymore. She hurried out from behind the wagon to find him. He stood at the edge of the camp while the men worked frantically in the distance to get the cattle back under control.

She ran toward him, terror ripping at her chest as a few cows that had gotten away from the herd raced directly toward him. He had his back to them, intent on watching the ones the men were herding into a circle, trying to force them to stop. He couldn't hear the others stampeding toward him.

Calling out, even though she knew he wouldn't

hear, she desperately tried to get her feet to move faster. But she knew she wouldn't get there in time.

Suddenly, from out of the cloud of dust, Logan barreled down toward Max, reaching down to grab him just before the cows reached him. They veered off in the other direction after being startled by the horse and rider. One of the other men chased after them, forcing them back toward the herd.

Falling to her knees, she choked on the dust as she tried to get her breathing back under control. She'd almost witnessed her brother being trampled to death, and she was sure her heart had ripped in half as she'd watched.

Burying her head in her hands, she let the tears flow as relief gripped her. Her shoulders shook as she sobbed. What would she have done if she'd lost her brother too?

Hearing hooves on the ground beside her, she looked up. Max leaped down from the horse, while Logan watched. Her brother ran into her arms, and they sat on the ground holding each other as she kissed the top of his head.

Before she could say anything to thank him, Logan had turned his horse around and was racing back into the open field. It seemed like the cattle had all been stopped quickly and hadn't actually managed to get very far.

But to her, it had felt like an eternity as she'd watched helplessly while the cows approached Max.

"Hurry up. Bring him over here," Logan's voice was yelling above the others as they came back toward the camp. Standing quickly, Hope realized someone was hurt. The men were on foot, carrying someone as they carefully came around the side of the wagon and placed him gently on the ground.

"Mr. O'Hara!" Hope raced over and knelt on the ground beside him.

"I'm fine, Miss. Just a little bump on my head." James took her hand and patted it as he tried to reassure her. Blood dripped from a cut near his ear, and he cringed as he tried to move slightly.

"Step back, Hope. Let Frank take a look." Logan reached down and pulled her up, as the cook came over and crouched down. He had a bag that looked like it contained basic medical supplies.

Max stood beside her, so she took his hand and squeezed it. Logan placed his hand on her shoulder and led her away. "Frank will get him fixed up. No sense you standing over top of him fretting."

She looked back and watched the cook wipe at the blood. "How will he know what to do? He isn't even a doctor."

"When you're on the trail, the cook is responsible for more than just feeding everyone. He's been on enough cattle drives to know what to do. This is likely the smallest one Frank has ever worked on, so he's used to more injuries happening than this."

They made their way over to the wagon where her new clothes still sat in the brown paper. Crossing her arms in front of her, she looked up at Logan. He was pretending not to worry, but she could see his eyes were back where James O'Hara was lying on the ground.

"What happened?"

Logan looked back at her as she spoke. He leaned back against the wagon bed and sighed. "He was coming around one side and one of the cows rammed into his horse, making it rear up. He fell hard and had to roll to avoid being trampled." He dragged his hat from his head and slammed it against his thighs. "I told the old fool to stay here and let us handle it, but he doesn't listen."

She could hear the concern and worry in Logan's voice, along with anger. But she could tell the anger wasn't aimed at James. "It's not your fault, Logan. I've only known Mr. O'Hara for a few days and I already know how stubborn he is. He wouldn't have listened to you anyway."

His eyes moved back to James. "No, he wouldn't. I just feel like I've got so many people counting on me, and I hate knowing he's hurt because of me. I should have been keeping a better eye on him."

Hope shook her head in disbelief. "Do you honestly believe you're supposed to be watching over everyone? You're one man, Logan. And if you hadn't been there to grab Max, I'd have been burying my brother too. You can't be everywhere."

Logan looked at Max who stood to the side, quietly watching them talk. She gasped as he moved his hands and asked Max how he was doing. The smile that spread across her brother's face reflected her own feelings. Logan had picked up some of the sign language and was speaking to Max.

Max signed back to say he wasn't hurt. Then he moved his hands and said thank you.

"How did you know how to sign?" Her voice shook with emotion.

"I've been watching you talk with him, and I've managed to figure some of the basic words." He shrugged nonchalantly, as though he hadn't just taken the time to learn something that would make a young child feel accepted.

Logan pushed himself away from the wagon. "I'm going to go check on James."

But before he walked away, he turned to face her. "It really isn't safe for you both out here. Max could have been killed today."

She knew what he was going to say next.

"You're not leaving us at the next town, Logan. I meant it when I said I'm paying you back. I know you feel like you're responsible for us, but you're not. I'm sorry that you've had the extra burden of us being with you, but I promise to do my part to help out and offer help when I can."

A knot was forming in her stomach as she thought about being left behind. And with a sudden jolt, she realized it wasn't just from fear of what would happen to her and her brother.

With a sinking feeling, she realized there was much more to it than that, and she wasn't sure what to do with the realization.

Because as she met Logan's blue eyes gazing into hers, she knew without a doubt it was him she'd be missing.

When he finally turned and walked toward the men huddled around James, Hope moved to lean against the wagon. Reaching down to move the brown paper on the forgotten package, she saw the handle of the brush just inside.

Her heart lurched as she wondered if this was what it felt like to be in love.

CHAPTER 12

"**Y**ou know yourself, you can't really complain about having them here. If it weren't for Hope, one of the men would have had to come off their duties to drive my wagon. And that boy has been earning his keep by helping anyone he can with all of the smaller tasks."

James had also broken his arm when he fell, and hadn't been able to drive the wagon for the past few days. Hope had stepped in, and with coaching from the older man, she was managing just fine.

Logan looked over to it now where Hope was hanging out a couple of shirts. One of the cowboys he'd hired was a bit smaller than the rest, and he'd offered Max some clothes to get him through to

Oregon. They were still a little big on him, but he just rolled up the sleeves and had been using a piece of rope as a belt.

Hope had run down to the small creek that was running past their camp to quickly wash some of the dusty clothes when they'd stopped for the day. She was even hanging out shirts that belonged to James, and some of the other men.

Smiling to himself, he had to laugh as he imagined what the men were thinking. He was pretty sure none of these cowboys he'd hired had ever had anyone do their laundry while on the trail.

Tomorrow they'd all be smelling like his mother's flowerbed.

"No, I agree. She's done a lot to help out around here. But what am I supposed to do with her and the boy when we get to Oregon? She's determined to pay me back, and I have no earthly idea how she intends to do that."

James grinned at him as he took another sip of his coffee. Luke chuckled quietly as he shook his head, quickly sipping from his own cup when Logan glared in his direction. "What exactly is it that you find so amusing?"

Luke shook his head and put his hand up in the air in mock surrender. "Nothing. Just that it seems to me you can't even see the simplest solution standing right in front of your own face."

Logan squinted at him, crossing his arms in front of his chest as he waited for Luke to elaborate. "Would you care to explain it to me then?"

Frank came over and bent down to pour some more coffee into Luke's cup. He turned to look at Logan with a serious expression.

"I think he's hinting at what the rest of us have all been able to see, even if your own eyes haven't been opened yet."

Rolling his eyes and sighing in exasperation, Logan shrugged. "All right then. Maybe one of you could let me know what has you all grinning like a bunch of fools."

Frank set the pot back on the fold-down shelf of the wagon. He turned back to Logan and looked him in the eye. "Well, what us fools have been able to see is that you're smitten with that woman."

Logan's jaw fell open, both at the accusation Frank had just aimed at him as well as the old, gruff cowboy's use of the word "smitten."

James and Luke were snickering like schoolboys.

"You're all crazy. I think we've been on the trail too long and perhaps you've all gone a little mad.

Because there's no way I'm *smitten*—" He glared over at Frank for emphasis before continuing, "—with Hope."

"There's nothing wrong with being attracted to a woman, Logan. That's how it's done." James sat with his arm in the sling, leaning back against the chuckwagon wheel.

"How what's done?" He was getting frustrated at the lack of information being provided.

James leaned slightly forward. "Well, when I first saw my dear Susan, I was drawn to her like a fly on cow dung."

Logan's eyebrow went up. "That's very poetic. I'm sure your wife loves to hear how you felt when you met her."

"Sometimes there's just a woman that draws you to her, and I can see that's what's happening with you and Hope. You can deny it all you want, but for the past three weeks on this trail, you've found every excuse you could to be around her. And whenever you're not, your eyes are looking for her."

Luke and Frank were both nodding in agreement. Standing up, Logan slammed his hat on his head and took his now empty cup to set by the bucket. "I've got work to do. I wish I could sit around and chit-chat with you old biddies, but someone needs to look after things around here."

He ignored the laughter behind him as he walked away. He was willing to admit there was something about Hope that did draw him to her, but it wasn't anything like they were letting on. She was pretty, there was no doubt about that. Every time she looked at him with her dark brown eyes, he did notice his pulse racing a bit.

But that didn't mean anything.

Besides, he was too young to be tied down with a woman. The last thing he wanted was to end up like his brothers, who were completely besotted and didn't even act like themselves anymore. Even his poor brother-in-law, Titus, wasn't the same man he was before he married Ella. Now it seemed they were all sitting around sipping tea with their wives under a tree every time he saw them.

He was far enough away from the others now, and able to look back to see what Hope was doing without them thinking he was some lovesick schoolboy. Crouching down, he started to untie his bedroll from the saddle lying on the ground. She was talking to one of the cowboys who'd come over to get his now clean shirt from her. Toby was smiling at her as he lifted his shirt to sniff it, then he bowed to her, taking his hat from his head in a wide sweeping gesture as he thanked her.

Logan raised his eyebrow. Did Toby seriously think he needed to be quite so dramatic with his thank you? And shouldn't he be out keeping an eye on the cows anyway? Logan was paying him to help get the cattle to Oregon, not spend his time flirting with the beautiful woman who was the only ray of sunshine on this dusty trail.

Sitting back on his heels, he cringed inwardly. Was he jealous? What was happening to him? Surely the others weren't right about what he was feeling for Hope.

Suddenly, she spotted him and waved before walking toward him. Standing up, Logan did his best to ignore the fact his heart was racing as her eyes met his.

He'd likely just stood up too fast. It had nothing to do with her.

"Logan, I was hoping I could have a word with you if you aren't too busy."

He nodded. "Sure, I'm just getting things ready to set out for tonight."

She put her hands out to him, holding one of his shirts. He hadn't even realized she'd washed it. "I washed this one for you. I saw it crumpled up in the back of the wagon so I thought maybe you'd like to get it freshened up."

He couldn't stop himself, and before he knew what he was doing, he was lifting it up to sniff it. He was no better than Toby, although he sure as lightning wasn't going to be gushing and bowing to thank her.

"It smells nice. Thank you."

She was standing still, watching him as she wrung her hands nervously in front of her. "I heard you telling Luke earlier that you were running into the fort that's set up near here in the morning."

He kept his eyes on hers and nodded warily. What did she want?

"I've got to go in and pick up a few supplies to get us the rest of the way to Oregon."

Her throat moved as she swallowed. "Well, I was just wondering if you could maybe take me with you? I've been thinking, and since I'm now eighteen, maybe I could try getting in touch with Sadie's lawyer. I'd like to see if I can get legal guardianship and not have to spend the rest of my life looking over my shoulder to see when she'll show up to take Max."

Logan brought his brows together in confusion. "I thought you said you weren't of age yet?"

She shrugged and gave him a bright smile. "I wasn't. But I am now. It would have been my birthday yesterday."

His eyebrows were still pulled together and his mouth was slightly open as he stared at her. It had been her birthday yesterday and she didn't even tell anyone?

He didn't know why he was surprised. Since the day they'd left Sacramento, she'd quietly gone about things without a complaint. She hadn't complained about sleeping on the hard ground, or when she'd only had one dress to wear. She ate the bland food that was normal with life on the trail, and she had never made a fuss that she'd only been able to wash in the cold water of creeks as they passed.

Most women would never have survived, yet Hope had never said a word.

And she'd known it was her birthday yesterday, but hadn't thought it was a big deal so didn't bother to mention it.

Blinking slowly, he brought his fingers up to rub the bridge of his nose. "Why didn't you tell me it was your birthday?"

She laughed and waved her hand dismissively. "It's not a big deal."

He shook his head and sighed. "Well, as for going into the fort, I don't think it's a good idea. If Sadie has sent anyone out looking for you or Max, it wouldn't be safe."

He didn't mention the fact that he'd already sent a wire back to Sacramento at the last town they'd passed. And it hadn't been to the lawyer. Logan had his suspicions and wasn't sure if the woman's lawyer would be truthful.

The sound of thunder rumbled in the distance, and lightning lit up the sky. Hope quickly turned her head to it. "I better get Max in for the night. He's afraid of storms."

She looked back at him. "Good night."

As she walked back to the wagon, with the sun almost down beyond the horizon, another flash of lightning tore across the sky illuminating the darkness of her hair. Her step faltered at the sound of the rumbling thunder, and she picked up her pace.

He was left standing there watching her, feeling the wind pick up around him. He wasn't sure if it was the storm coming that was playing with his mind, or if he'd just realized the truth he'd been trying to deny.

The sudden urge to run after her and hold her in his arms until the storm passed, took over him. He had to turn and look away.

As he did, his eyes met those of James O'Hara smiling back at him. The older man shrugged then slowly walked away.

Logan knew exactly what he was thinking.

And as another flash of lightning lit up the sky, Logan realized he might just be right.

CHAPTER 13

*H*ope held Max close, listening as the wind whipped the canvas that was tied around their makeshift tent. Even with the full load of supplies, the wagon they cowered under moved with the force of the storm, creaking and groaning with every blast of wind that hit it. The small lantern she had lit was the only comfort from the fury of the weather outside.

She could hear the men hollering to each other while they rushed to secure the camp as the rain started to fall around them.

Suddenly, the canvas was pulled back and Logan's head peered inside. Water dripped from the brim of his hat. "James is going to stay here with you both while we stand guard to keep the cattle from spooking again." He moved aside and the older man crawled inside. She quickly moved to make more room for him.

"Of course, you're more than welcome under here where its dry, Mr. O'Hara. It's your wagon, and if not for us, you'd have been able to use it as shelter." Guilt hit her as she realized while her and Max had been sitting here sheltered from the storm brewing outside, the rest were forced to stay out in it.

"Nonsense. If not for this arm of mine, I'd be out helping keep the cattle under control." He looked at Logan and she noticed him scowl at James. "But this young whip here thinks it's safer for me to stay here where I can't get hurt again."

"I don't need to be worrying about you if those cows get moving again. With the thunder and wind, it's a good possibility. So I'd rather you stay here and keep Hope and Max safe." Logan was already backing away from the opening in the canvas. "I'll be back to check on you later."

The canvas fell back down as he ran into the darkness, leaving them in the shelter of the flickering lantern.

"He'll be fine. Logan Wallace is so stubborn I'm sure even Mother Nature herself couldn't win a fight against him." James reached out and patted her arm. She hadn't even realized she'd been left staring at the opening where she'd last seen Logan. Feeling heat rise in her cheeks, she turned and smiled at the man.

"I know. I've noticed that about him." She smoothed at her skirts, trying not to hear the sounds of the storm raging outside. Max was more relaxed now that James was there, so he'd curled up on his blanket next to her. Even though he couldn't hear the thunder, the lightning always scared him. So she was grateful the older man was here to give her brother some comfort.

Reaching her hand down, she brushed at his hair with her fingers. She looked down at the dark hair, so soft on the head of a boy still so young and innocent. Thoughts and worries rushed into her mind as she realized once more that after this trip was over, they were on their own again.

"You know, things always seem to have a way of working out for the best. You've just got to have faith that something better is on the way to you."

James's voice broke into her thoughts, startling her. She looked up and met his gaze. How did he always seem to know what to say? She remembered a time when her father was like that. It was so long ago, she almost thought she was imagining it.

"I hope you're right, Mr. O'Hara."

Just as she was about to spill all her worries onto his shoulders, a loud crash could be heard outside. He moved toward the canvas, quickly pulling it back with his good arm. The wagon was swaying wildly above them, and the sound of the rain hitting the ground outside sounded louder than the thunder rolling in the sky.

Max sat up, crawling closer to her and letting her put her arm around his shoulders as they watched James move out into the shadows.

Suddenly, a large gust of wind blew the canvas off from the back of the wagon, taking the light from the lantern in a puff of smoke. Darkness wrapped around them, and Max's arms gripped her tighter. A loud crack of thunder echoed over- head, vibrating the ground they sat on.

Another piece of the canvas tore from the side, letting the fury of the rain blast inside. She had to try covering it back up to keep Max dry, but she had no way to let him see her to tell him what she was going to do.

When she moved to go outside, he clawed at her, desperately trying to make her stay. She patted his hand, trying to let him know she'd be right back. But she knew he wasn't going to let her leave without him, so she just took his hand and led him out from under the wagon. Looking around, she struggled in the blackness to try finding the canvas. The rain soaked through her clothes instantly, and she had to wipe at her eyes as the drops beat against her face.

The lightning was almost constant now, giving her time to see between bursts as she made her way around the wagon. She could make out a broken crate lying on the ground, broken pieces of wood all around the white, gooey substance it had held. "Mr. O'Hara?" She called out the man's name into the raging wind, hoping he wasn't hurt.

Shielding her eyes, she squinted into the rain, her hair blowing out behind her. Where had he gone?

When the sky lit up once more, the outline of the man could be seen struggling against something next to the wagon. As she moved toward him, Max suddenly broke free from her grasp, racing ahead of her. He got to the man and pushed him hard just as another box fell from the wagon.

In shock, Hope watched as the box hit her brother, knocking him onto the ground. James grabbed the box with his good arm, throwing it off Max as he crouched down beside him. She knelt on the other side, desperately feeling with her hands to see where he was hurt.

"I think it knocked him out. I can't lift him. Stay here until I can go find someone to help." James shouted to her as he stood back up, moving as fast as his legs would take him into the darkness.

The rain still pounded, hiding the tears that were pouring down her cheeks. Her hands caressed his soft cheeks as she leaned over him, trying to shelter him from the worst of the storm.

After what seemed like an eternity, she felt a hand on her shoulder, pulling her back. Logan reached down and lifted him, carrying him back to the shelter of the wagon. He called out behind him as he crouched down, "Luke, find something to cover this wagon back up."

She crawled back under, helping Logan to pull Max into the corner that still had some shelter. "What happened? Why were you out there?" Logan's voice was angry as he tried to get the lantern to light again. Finally, a small spark flickered to life, showing the white face of her brother lying on the ground between them.

A trail of blood wound down his forehead, and

a dark bruise had already formed along his hairline.

Luke and James managed to get the canvas secured back up, keeping the wind and rain outside. James crawled back under, using his good arm to move forward. "How is he?"

Logan shook his head as he pulled Max's hair back to get a better look.

"I can't tell. He's still unconscious." Logan lifted his eyes and met Hope's. Rain dripped from the brim of his hat, so he quickly ripped it from his head, pushing his hand through his wet hair. "I told you to stay under the wagon. I can't be worrying about you two when I'm doing everything else."

Her body shook from the coldness that was soaking into her bones, but also from fear for her brother. And now, she was being scolded like a child.

Something snapped inside her. "We went out to get the canvas to put back over the sides. We weren't going out in the storm just to annoy you. I wanted to go out by myself to fix our shelter—that was all. But unfortunately, he was scared, so wouldn't let go of me and had to come too. I know you don't want the extra responsibility of having us here, and we've been a burden on you since the first day you found us, so I assure you, as soon as we get to Oregon, we'll be on our way."

She leaned over and kissed her brother's pale cheek so Logan couldn't see the tears streaming down her cheeks.

"He pushed me out of the way, Logan. If he hadn't, that box would have hit me. He was trying to protect me." James's voice gruffly spoke above her. "I'd gone out and left them alone, so if you're going to be yelling at anyone, you should be aiming your words at me."

She didn't want to look at him, so she stayed over her brother, dabbing at the blood with the edge of the blanket.

"I'm going to find Frank. Stay here with them." Logan's voice sounded strained as he moved away from the other side of Max.

The storm was finally letting up, and as she heard the canvas pull back, she realized the rain had slowed down to a trickle outside.

A hand reached out and touched her shoulder. "He'll be all right, Hope." She could hear the pain and guilt in James's voice.

She wanted to tell the man it wasn't his fault, but at the moment, words wouldn't come to her. All she could do was pray he was right.

he sun had beat down on them all day, quickly drying up the mud and puddles that covered the ground. When Max had woken up with nothing more than a bad headache, relief had swept through the camp. The boy had managed to soften even the hardest hearts over the days on the trail, so when news had spread that he'd been hurt, everyone had been worried.

They'd waited until noon to move out, taking the morning to clean up the camp and repair some of the damage. James had lost another crate of flour, so Logan figured at this rate, he'd have none left by the time they reached Oregon.

Hope wouldn't speak more than a few words to him this morning, and truthfully, he couldn't blame her. In his anger last night, he'd made her feel like she was a burden. He'd just been so scared when James had found him and said Max had been hurt. Then seeing him lying on the ground like that had sent fear rippling through his body.

Now, as the camp settled down for the night, Logan was left standing against a tree at the side of the camp with only the fire to keep him company. Sleep hadn't come easily last night after the storm, so everyone had turned in early. He'd offered to take the first watch tonight, knowing he wouldn't be able to sleep anyway.

He had to keep his eye on the cattle, protecting them from any predators that might threaten them, as well as keeping watch on the wagon where Hope slept. The moon was bright tonight, lighting up sky with a blue glow that cast shadows on the trees and hills in the distance.

An owl called out in the distance, interrupted only by the crackling of the fire that burned low giving warmth to the men sleeping around it.

His eyes kept moving to the wagon, wishing he could talk to Hope. As though his thoughts could bring things into being, the woman he was thinking about stepped around the side of the wagon, her eyes meeting his.

She stood still, and he almost thought she was

going to turn and go back under the wagon. Finally, she moved toward him.

She wrapped her arms around herself as she came to a stop in front of him. "I'm sorry for raising my voice last night. You've done so much for me, and it wasn't fair for me to yell at you like that."

He shook his head. "No, I'm the one who should apologize. I didn't mean to make you feel like you were a burden on me. I was just a bit shook up to see Max hurt like that, so I guess I took it out on you."

She lifted her eyes, and the breath flew from his lungs as he found himself lost in her gaze. His feet were moving before he could stop himself and he stopped right in front of her. Her head tipped up, and his hand moved out to touch her cheek.

With a sinking feeling, he knew he was lost with no chance of ever coming back.

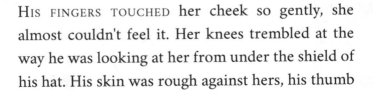

His fingers touched her cheek so gently, she almost couldn't feel it. Her knees trembled at the way he was looking at her from under the shield of his hat. His skin was rough against hers, his thumb moving tenderly along the edge of her jaw. His eyes moved to follow everywhere he touched, leaving a trail of heat as he went.

Swallowing, she tried to remind herself to breathe. Her eyes closed as he took his hand and slid it down her neck. His fingers tickled the soft skin, before moving back up, and his thumb made a line across her lip.

Opening her eyes slightly, she was just in time to see his head start to lower. Their eyes met and she leaned into him, urging him to continue.

She knew she was acting wantonly and it wasn't at all proper to be standing out here kissing a man. But after the events of the past few weeks, she figured she was beyond caring what was right or wrong.

All she knew was this man had weaved a spell around her, and she was helpless to fight it.

When his lips touched hers, she had to bring her hands up to hold onto his jacket as her legs started to buckle. Thankfully, his other hand wrapped tightly around her waist, pressing her to him.

As his lips moved, his fingers continued the assault on her senses. He tenderly caressed the skin on her jaw, circling down to her neck and back up until she was sure the dizziness she was feeling was going to take over.

Her skin tingled everywhere his fingers brushed, and where they were pressed together, she was certain she felt his heart beating against hers.

Finally, he pulled back slightly, looking down as she fought to open her eyes. Her lips were still parted and she wanted to cry out, telling him to continue.

He smiled and brought his fingers up to brush her hair back, tucking it behind her ear.

"I suppose I shouldn't have done that." His voice was husky, sounding loud in the quiet of the night around them.

She smiled back, her fingers still firmly gripped around the collar of his jacket. "And I suppose I shouldn't have let you."

His eyes went to her lips again, and she sucked in her breath, holding it as she waited to see if he was going to continue. She realized with a jolt how badly she hoped he would.

A noise behind her made him lift his gaze and look past her.

"It looks like we've been caught," he whispered the words in her ear as he raised his eyebrows. He loosened his grip, not letting go completely, so she could turn around.

There stood Max, watching them with a look of disgust on his face.

"What are you doing?" He signed the question as he walked over to them.

Her cheeks were hot with embarrassment at what her brother had seen them doing. She tried to pull away, but Logan still held his hands on her arms as she stood in front of him.

"I was just talking with Mr. Wallace," she signed back.

Max crinkled his eyes together. "Why were you kissing him?" She could see his ten-year-old mind didn't think kissing was something he'd ever want to be doing.

Logan's chest rumbled behind her as he laughed to himself. Obviously, he'd been able to figure out what Max had asked and found it quite humorous.

She pulled herself out of his grip and walked to Max, turning to scowl at Logan. She wasn't finding this amusing at all, in fact, she was mortified that her brother had caught them.

But Logan just shrugged, not offering her any help as to what to say.

"Come on, Max, let's get you back to bed. You've had a long day." She avoided answering his question, taking him by the shoulders to turn him around. Max gave a quick look over his shoulder at Logan, but let her lead him back around the other side of the wagon.

She ignored the quiet chuckling sound coming from Logan as they walked away.

Crawling back underneath the wagon, she tucked her brother in tightly. He looked up at her with a smile. "I like, Mr. Wallace. It's all right if you were kissing him."

Just when she was sure her face couldn't heat up anymore, it burned with embarrassment again. "Go to sleep."

That was all she could think to say to him. Max grinned at her, then closed his eyes as he snuggled into his blankets. The moon was so bright tonight, it was still light enough to see everything, and she sat looking down into the face she loved so much. He had a nice bruise on his forehead, and a gash where the box had hit it, but thankfully he didn't seem to have any other problems from it.

She needed to remember what was important, and that was looking after Max and making sure he was safe. She couldn't be out standing in the moonlight kissing a man who wasn't even her husband.

Besides, Logan had never given any hint that he wanted them to stick around when they got to Oregon. In fact, he had mentioned on more than one occasion she was free to leave when they got there and she wasn't indebted to him.

Taking her blanket, she wrapped it around herself as she lay back down. The ground seemed even harder tonight as she struggled to get comfortable. Knowing Logan was standing just a few feet away on the other side of the canvas was unsettling. Remembering the way his fingers moved over her skin gave her an ache in her chest.

It had felt like he truly cared for her. Surely that wasn't something she could just be imagining.

As she looked up at the bottom of the wagon, the sounds of steady breathing coming from her brother beside her, her thoughts were all in a jumble.

She knew they'd be in Oregon soon, and she still didn't know what they'd do when they got there. She still intended to pay Logan back some-how. James had told her he'd sold a couple of the cows he'd been bringing back at one of the little towns they'd camped near. He was going to use that money to give to his sister for what he'd spent on her. So, she knew she had to repay him for doing that.

But how could she stay around him now, knowing how she was feeling?

After what had happened tonight, she no longer had any doubts. She'd fallen in love with Logan Wallace, and she had to figure out how she could walk away once she'd repaid him.

The thought of it already made her heart ache.

CHAPTER 15

*D*ust hung in the air as they made their way the final few miles to his homestead. They'd managed to make good time the last day, as though the cattle and the men all knew the long trip was almost over. The familiar landmarks around his family's land gave him a feeling of peace knowing they were home.

In the distance, he could make out the cropping of trees where Titus and Ella lived. He was just on the other side of their property, in the land he'd purchased when the former owner had been arrested on charges of murder.

It was nice to have a place of his own, after living on the original homestead with his mother while his older brothers built their own homes. They all still farmed together and now, between all of them, they owned a large portion of the land just outside Bethany.

But this place, this small little parcel, was all his. And he'd been excited to get the cattle he wanted to start his own herd. Seeing the small house just ahead, his chest swelled with pride. It wasn't much, but to him it was paradise.

For some reason, he found himself turning his head to see if he could tell what Hope was thinking. She was holding the reins to James's wagon, while the older man pointed and talked to her, obviously telling her they were about to arrive at Logan's.

The sound of the cattle's hooves were heavy on the dirt road as they got closer. It seemed as though they sensed they would soon be able to rest, so were moving faster than they'd done the entire trip.

His eyes moved around him, and he breathed deeply. Everything around him was familiar. The trees lining the road, the long grass blowing in the breeze, and the lush crops he'd helped his brothers plant before leaving were standing tall, soon ready to be taken off the fields.

Riding ahead, he leaped down from his horse to open the gate to the pen he'd put up to hold the cattle when they arrived home. He'd sort them after they'd had a chance to settle and put them into the pasture around the property.

Hope pulled the wagon to the far side by the small house, while the men herded the cows into the pen. Frank had already headed into Bethany, saying there was no use for him on the final leg of the trip. The rest would meet up with him for a well-deserved rest.

Logan would have to head in too and pay them all. As he stood at the corner of the pen watching his herd run inside amid the calls of the cowboys, he turned to look at Hope. She was still sitting in the wagon, holding the reins and looking all around her. Max had hopped down right after James, and was running over to stand by Logan to watch the cows be put into the pen.

He knew she'd grown up in a far fancier home than what she was seeing here, so he wondered what she was thinking. Most likely, she was contemplating how she could hurry and pay him back so she could be on her way to somewhere more civilized.

He still didn't know what to do with her. He'd agonized over it for the past week, since they'd shared a kiss.

Even now, when he thought about that night, his chest ached. He'd never wanted to let her go.

He knew she was embarrassed, and had been trying to keep her distance from him ever since, but he couldn't stop thinking about it.

He couldn't stop thinking about *her*.

As the last cow went through the gate, he closed it, turning to thank the men who'd helped him make the trip. He told them to head into town to Dorothy Larsen's boardinghouse to get cleaned up and have a rest. She'd take care of them, and he'd be sure to pay for their rooms when he came to pay them.

Watching them race out of the yard, headed to town, Logan had to smile. These men hired on to do cattle drives worked hard. But when the drive was over, they knew how to kick their boots up and have some fun.

He just hoped Bethany was ready for them.

James was showing Max around the farm, and the boy had already found one of the wild barn cats that hung around. He was crouched down trying to catch the black bundle of fur.

Hope still sat in the wagon, not moving. He walked toward her, putting his hand out to help her down.

"Aren't you going to get down and stretch your legs? That last bit of the trip was a bit longer, but I didn't think there was much sense in stopping for lunch when we were so close to home."

Her eyes were following Max as he followed along behind James. He had somehow managed to catch the cat, and was carrying it wrapped in his arms.

Finally, she smiled down at him, but it didn't reach her eyes. "So, now what do we do? I have no money, and no way of taking care of Max until I can find a job. And I need to find somewhere that can support me, plus pay you what I owe."

He knew she'd been worried, and obviously had been thinking the same thoughts as he had.

"Hope, I told you I wasn't just going to abandon you when we got here. And I swear, if I hear you talk about paying me back one more time, I'm going to take you straight back to Sadie's and leave you on her doorstep."

Her eyes grew wide and she gasped loudly. "You wouldn't!"

He shrugged. He knew without a doubt he'd never do that, but he was tired of her insisting she had to pay him back. Honestly, the girl was more stubborn than his sister Ella.

Before they could continue their conversation, he heard a wagon coming up the lane. Voices loudly called out his name, and he turned to see what appeared to be the entire family making their way over.

He'd known they'd be watching for him, and as soon as they'd come down the road, he had no doubt they'd have heard the commotion. But he thought maybe they'd wait at least a few minutes before circling in on him.

Of course, he should have known better. The Wallace's were a fiercely tight family, and when one came home after being gone a while, there wouldn't be any waiting to see them.

Looking up at Hope, she was watching the wagon pull in, with the others on horseback riding alongside. As he saw the look of shock on her face at the sudden intrusion, he grinned.

"Well, Hope, I guess it's time to meet my family."

She stood, reaching up to try patting her hair into some semblance of order. She wiped at her face, trying desperately to get at least one layer of the dust off. He reached up to help her down, grabbing her around the waist as she leaned over to take his hand, and spinning her onto the ground.

"Logan, what will everyone think?" She was mortified as she reached down to rub the creases out of her skirt.

He didn't have time to answer as a small body flung herself at him. Picking her up, he spun around, laughing at the young girl who was squealing with happiness. "Oh, Sophia, I think you grew all the way up while I was gone!" Reid's daughter seemed to have sprouted up by at least two feet.

"No, I didn't." She wrapped her arms around his neck, squeezing tightly.

"Logan, aren't you even going to offer your poor old mother a hug?" He grinned as he set Sophia down, then pulled his mother in for a hug, lifting her and spinning her around too.

"Logan Wallace, put me down. For heaven's sake, you're apt to drop me." She tapped him hard on the shoulder.

"Luke!"

Luke had been walking up from the pen when he saw the wagon pull in, and his sisters had just noticed him. Phoebe and Grace were racing to him, almost knocking him to the ground when they got there.

Everyone else took their turns slapping him on

the back and hugging him as though he'd been missing for years, and not just a few weeks.

"So, it seems you've got a few extra people than you left with." Colton looked over at Hope. Max had come over when everyone arrived, and was now shyly hanging onto her arm.

"Logan Wallace, you better not have gone off and got yourself married without telling us." His mother went over and took Hope's hands in hers. "Hello, dear, welcome to Bethany."

Rolling his eyes, he wished at this moment he had a slightly smaller and less intrusive family. Hope looked ready to run, obviously uncomfortable at now being the center of their attention.

"No, Ma, I didn't get married. Hope and her brother needed a hand, so I helped them out."

Ella was standing beside him, and she was looking around the yard. "So, where's the mare you were bringing back for me?"

His head turned, and he saw the panic in Hope's eyes. Everyone was now about to find out what had happened. She was probably worried about how they were going to react.

"Well, it's kind of a funny story..."

CHAPTER 16

"*O*h, you poor girl. What you've been through. And your brother. I've never in my life been so angry at a stranger. So help me, if your stepmother ever shows her face around this town, don't you worry. We'll take care of you." Anna Wallace's bright blue eyes looked at her with compassion as she reached across the table and held her hand.

"We don't know for sure, but I wouldn't put it past the woman to show up here. Or at least send her hired thugs here. I just can't see her giving up that easily." Logan was leaning against the wall next to his brothers, while the women sat at the table in his small home.

"Well, you and your brother will be coming to stay with me. And I won't hear you argue."

Logan pushed away from the wall, and reached into his pocket. He took the money out and handed it to Titus.

His sister's husband looked at the money and shook his head. "No, you don't owe us anything. You did the right thing with that money. If I'd have found out you'd walked out and left a girl to face that fate instead of helping her, you'd have been seeing stars for days.

"Please take it. I feel terrible that he spent your money. And now he's sold some of his own cows to pay it back, and I'd feel terrible knowing he did that too. I don't know how I'll ever repay everything, but please, don't let me be any more indebted to you," Hope pleaded with Ella. That way, she'd only have to pay off her debt to him. She couldn't stand knowing she owed them too.

Ella looked at Logan, and he just shrugged. "I've been telling her for weeks she doesn't owe me anything, but unfortunately when it comes to being stubborn, I'm afraid she even has you beat."

Ella made a face at her brother, then took the money from his hand.

The sound of laughter outside, pulled her eyes to the window next to the table. Max was racing around, with Sophia trying to catch up to him.

Phoebe and Luke's younger sister, Grace, stood off to the side laughing with them. She was a bit older than the rest of them, but she was having fun watching them run around the yard.

James had left, saying he was sure he could manage to drive the team of horses as far as town. She was already missing him, and even old Frank too. They'd become familiar to her, and the only one she knew in this room was Logan.

"Let's get you home so you can rest. I remember what it was like sleeping on the trail, so I know you'll appreciate a soft mattress to lie on tonight." Anna stood, while the rest of the family started to move toward the doorway. Suddenly feeling panicked, she met Logan's eyes.

He looked a bit confused too. They'd just spend a month together on the trail, and the thought of leaving him right now made her chest tighten. But that was silly. Mrs. Wallace had offered Max and her a home to stay in until they could figure out where they'd go. She couldn't refuse the offer.

And staying with Logan wouldn't be appropriate for an unmarried woman.

Walking toward the wagon, Reid's wife, Audrey, touched her on the arm. "I have some clothing that will fit you for now. I'm not as tall as the other women in this family, so they should be more your size." She smiled at Hope. "I'll send Reid over with them."

A lump was forming in her throat as everyone seemed to be speaking at once. Everyone was being so kind and welcoming, and she'd never thought she would ever be around people like this again.

But all she wanted right now was a few minutes to say goodbye to Logan. From now on, they wouldn't have any chances to be alone. He stood back, watching everyone milling around, climbing back into the wagons and onto the horses. Max came over to stand beside him.

Logan looked at her with pain in his eyes as he tried to explain to Max that they'd be staying somewhere else. He faltered on some of the signs, looking to her for help. Walking over to Max, she told him they'd be staying at Mrs. Wallace's until they figured out where to go.

Tears formed in his eyes as he looked up at Logan. Logan crouched down. "Tell him not to worry, he'll still see me all the time. And I still want him to come help me over here, like we talked about."

Her heart ached as she saw the sadness in her

brother's face. He'd hoped they would be staying with Logan, not realizing it wouldn't be considered proper.

Max flung himself into Logan's arms, and Hope swallowed hard, trying to get rid of the lump.

Logan stood back up and Max came over by her. She sensed that the rest of the family were making themselves busy elsewhere so they could say goodbye.

"You'll like staying with my ma. She'll make sure you guys are well fed. And I'm sure she'll enjoy the company. I'm over there quite a bit, as are the rest of the family, so you'll be kept busy."

She nodded. "But how will I be able to earn the money—"

He put his hand up and shook his head angrily. "No more talking about the money, Hope. I mean it. Just worry about taking care of Max."

She knew she would still see him. It wasn't like she was going hundreds of miles away. But knowing she wouldn't be around him every day was turning out to be harder for her to accept than she'd realized.

She wanted to at least give him a hug. After everything he'd done for her, she didn't think it right to just walk away. But with everyone watching, she couldn't bring herself to move.

"Thank you, Logan. For everything."

He nodded, then winked from under the shield of his hat, setting her cheeks on fire. "You're not getting rid of me that easy. I'll see you tomorrow at church."

He walked her over to Reid's wagon, taking her hand to help her up into the box at the back. Because his family often travelled together, benches lined each side of the box. Ella reached out to help steady her as she climbed in. Logan then turned and lifted Max in behind her.

Pasting a smile on her face, she tried to ignore the pain she was feeling. Even though he'd said himself, they'd see each other tomorrow, she felt everything had changed.

They were no longer alone on the trail, and he could go back to his life.

She was going to have to move on somehow.

Everyone talked around her, all so happy Logan was home, and welcoming Hope and Max into their fold. Colton and Titus rode their horses alongside the wagon, and Reid and Anna sat up front on the seat. The women, babies, and children all rode in the back.

Ella was seated across from her, watching her closely as she held her baby in her arms. Logan's sister had the same bright blue eyes he did, as did both of his brothers. Tilting her blonde head slightly, Ella creased her brows together. "You know, I've never quite seen my little brother so taken with a woman."

Hope laughed nervously. "No, it's wasn't like that. He was just helping me get away from a bad situation. He was being kind, that's all."

This time Ella laughed. Phoebe leaned over and looked back to where Logan was still standing, watching the wagon bounce down the road. Leaning back, she nodded. "I have to say, I agree with Ella. I've known Logan for long enough to see the difference in him. When he left Oregon, he was a young man with no responsibility or obligations. He enjoyed making fun of his brother's, and Titus, who he believed had become soft when they fell in love and married. But I noticed how he watched you, and you might not notice it yourself, but everyone around you both could feel it. I'd say if you were willing to give him the chance, he just might sweep you off your feet."

Hope's gaze turned back to see Logan still standing there. Luke was staying to help him get the animals settled, then was headed to Phoebe's. But Luke had gone back to the pen and right now, Logan stood alone. It was all she could do not to yell for them to stop the wagon so she could run back to him.

She knew she couldn't do that, though. Other than the kiss they'd shared, and the fact that these women believed it to be true, Logan had never given her any signs that he might care for her in that way.

Even if she knew what she was feeling in her own heart.

CHAPTER 17

"You know, you're making even more a fool of yourself by acting like you don't care about her at all. You spent the entire service today with your eyes stuck to the back of her head."

Logan rolled his eyes at Colton, as his brother and Luke chuckled to themselves. They stood outside the church, waiting for everyone to finish visiting so they could head out to Reid and Audrey's for their Sunday family picnic. Everyone was so excited to meet someone new in town, so Hope and Max were over with the women, being introduced to everyone.

They'd decided to keep the details of how they'd ended up here to themselves, introducing them as old family friends who'd been sent to Bethany after their parents passed away.

No one needed to know any more than that.

He leaned against the wagon, looking out over the top. His foot rested on the wheel, and as he watched, Max spotted him standing there and waved excitedly. He motioned with his head for the boy to come over, and Max didn't waste any time breaking free from the group of women.

Hope looked panicked for a moment as Max let go of her hand and ran away, until she saw where he was headed. She smiled shyly and turned back to speak to the women she'd just met.

He crouched down slightly as Max ran over, letting the boy give him a hug. When he pulled back, he asked Max if he'd slept well. At least he hoped he was using the signs correctly, and that's what he was asking him. He'd spent a great deal of time watching and learning along the trail, so he was fairly confident with some of the easier words.

When Max replied that he did, but that he missed him, Logan's chest hurt. He'd kind of missed having Max around last night too. He knew without a doubt he'd missed having Hope nearby, and he'd spent the night tossing and turning. He was finally sleeping in a comfortable bed, but he may as well have been back on the ground.

He had finally admitted to himself that what his brothers, and everyone else for that matter, were saying. And he'd decided he was going to do whatever he had to do to win Hope's heart. Even if he did end up becoming soft like his brothers. For Hope, it would be worth it.

But he wasn't going to give them the satisfaction of telling them that yet. He knew he was going to face terrible teasing from everyone for the amount of ribbing he'd given each of them.

It was a beautiful day in Bethany, and as he stood waiting for everyone to finish, he realized just how much he'd missed home. The town was small, and other than those who stood in front of the church, there was no one else milling around on the streets.

Nothing at all like Sacramento.

As he looked around, though, his eyes caught someone standing across the grass, to the side of the boardinghouse. He was looking in their direction, with his hat pulled down as he leaned against the building, arms crossed in front of him. A chill went down his spine as he watched and saw two more men step around the side and join the other man.

He turned to find Luke who was on the other side of the wagon, bugging his youngest sister.

"Luke, we've got a problem." Luke stopped and came over, while Titus, Colton and Reid stepped over too. They'd obviously picked up the concern in Logan's voice.

Logan tilted his head toward the boardinghouse. "Looks like Mr. Clarence Harding didn't give up the search after all."

Luke cursed softly under his breath when he recognized the man. Logan had no doubt Clarence had already seen Max who was still standing to the side.

Quickly explaining to his brothers who the men were, Logan kept his eyes on Hope, not wanting her to realize the situation that was unfolding. They made a plan to go over and talk to the men, and hopefully not worry the women.

Logan motioned to Max, then signed to tell him to wait here and he'd be right back. When they got across the field to the boardinghouse, Logan had to hold his anger in check when he saw the smirk on the man's face.

"You likely thought you'd seen the last of old Clarence, didn't you?" Clarence was still leaning against the wall like he didn't have a care in the world.

"Well, I was hoping. There's nothing for you here, so you and your men can keep moving."

Logan shook with anger. His brothers, Titus and Luke were lined up on either side of him, and as they stood there, he noticed James O'Hara making his way across the grass toward them. They might not be gunslingers like these men, but if it came down to it, he knew they'd all be willing to fight to keep Max from being taken by these men.

Clarence laughed slowly and quietly. He was one of those men who believed no harm could ever come to him as long as he had his hired thugs standing close by.

"Oh, I'd like nothing more than that. I'd like to get back down to California. The weather up here isn't near as pleasant. But I've got a job to do, and I'm not the kinda man who leaves a job unfinished."

From behind him, he heard Hope's voice, and cringed knowing the fool woman had seen what was happening and couldn't just stay put.

"You're not taking my brother, so if you think you're going to lay one filthy hand on him, you obviously don't have the sense God gave you."

Taking a deep breath, Logan turned to give Hope a look that told her to stay back and not speak another word. She stopped beside James and glared at Clarence.

This time, Clarence laughed even louder. "Oh, she's a feisty one. I can see why the old woman wanted to get her out of her hair."

Clarence finally pushed himself away from the wall and lifted his hat enough to see his eyes. "You can all rest easy. It's the Lord's day, and I'm not here to cause any trouble. The lady who hired me is on her way here to escort her stepson back to California. I'm just supposed to make sure you don't run off with him. She should be here by tomorrow."

When Hope gasped out loud, Clarence turned to grin at her. "You didn't think I believed you didn't have the boy with you, did you? Oh, I knew he was there, but the longer I put off finding him, the more I get paid. So, I've been following along and sent a message to the woman to let her know I'd found him days ago."

Clarence pulled the brim of his hat down and

turned, the men beside him following him around to the front of the street. Logan stood watching them go, the muscles in his jaw clenching as he struggled to figure out what he was going to do now.

Hope ran up to him, taking his arm and turning him to her. "What are we going to do?" The fear in her eyes tore at his heart.

"I promise you, Sadie won't get her hands on Max." Just as he was about to pull her into his arms, Ella raced over from where the rest of them had stayed over by the church. "Logan...Max is gone."

Dread formed in the pit of his stomach.

"He saw everyone over here, and took off in the other direction before any of us realized what was going on. He must have known something was up."

Logan raced back to the wagon, looking all around for a sign of the boy. Clarence was still in town, and the last thing he needed was for that man to find Max.

Within moments, the Wallace men, Luke Hamilton, Titus, and even Ella were on horses borrowed from the livery up the street. A few other men from town had hopped on their own and were taking instructions on where to look and what to do if they found him.

All Logan could do was pray they got to him before anyone else did.

CHAPTER 18

"I won't be able to sleep, Logan. Please, we have to keep looking." Desperately, she pleaded with him to keep going. His arms were around her, holding the reins as they rode through the bushes. Since she couldn't ride on her own, she'd gone with him. She'd been adamant she wasn't being left out of the search.

"Maybe one of the others has had more luck. It won't hurt to check." If anyone found Max, they were to meet at Anna's. They'd been checking in every couple of hours since they started searching, and so far, no one had found a sign of him.

It made it hard when they couldn't call out to him, and knowing Clarence was still around, while Max hid in unfamiliar territory made them all uneasy. Not to mention the fact it was now almost completely dark, and other than the faint light from the moon, Max would be alone and scared without any way of finding his way back.

Her stomach was coiled in knots as she imagined him on his own in the dark. "Why didn't I stay there with him? I had to be hot-headed and go down there to confront Clarence, instead of staying where I should have been. He wouldn't have run if I'd been there."

She had been angry with herself all day, knowing Max had got scared when he saw her down there with all the men. The poor child knew he could be taken away in a heartbeat, and his first instinct was now to just run before they could get him.

"Well, I'm not going to argue on the part about being hot-headed or the fact you should have stayed where you were." She stiffened as he started to speak, but he brought his arms in tighter and pulled her back to rest against his chest. "But it wasn't your fault he ran, Hope. The poor kid is terrified, and even if you'd been there, he would have run."

His chest vibrated against her back as he spoke. Every muscle in her body ached from being bounced on the back of the horse for hours. After the first hour, she'd finally let herself lean into Logan, no longer caring if it was proper or not. She was scared, tired, and just wanted to find her brother.

As they approached the edge of the bush leading into Anna's yard, she could see the others standing around. There was no sign of Max. Gently tugging on the reins, he brought the horse to stop.

"It's so dark, Logan. He can't stay out here all night by himself." Her words were spoken barely above a whisper.

He brought his arms around her and held her tighter to him, resting his chin on the top of her head. "He won't be out here alone, Hope. I'm going to keep looking. And I know my brothers. They'll be out here too. But you need to get some rest. You won't do any good if you're out here worrying."

Her body shook as she fought against the emotions of the day. He moved slightly to the side, letting her lean into his arm as he turned her slightly to face him. "I will find him. I promise."

She looked into his face, seeing the worry in his eyes. Logan cared about Max, so she had no fear that he'd give up looking for him.

All she could do was nod, no longer able to

speak against the pain in her throat as she fought back the tears. Once again, Logan was having to step in and help them. She didn't know what she'd have done if he hadn't come into their lives.

He pulled her back into him and kicked the horse into motion. They rode into the light cast by the lantern hanging by the doorway, while everyone rushed over.

These people—strangers only weeks ago—had spent the day looking for Max. They'd all worked together to help. And somehow knowing they were all here, not willing to give up yet, and so sure they'd find Max before too long, gave her the strength she needed to believe it too.

～

LOGAN PUSHED BACK the branches as he made his way back over the same trail he'd searched a hundred times already. Where would Max have gone? He'd been out all night, as had all the others. There wasn't a sign of him anywhere.

He pushed the thoughts from his head that Clarence had found him first.

As the sky started to lighten and a pink hue spread across the horizon, Logan's stomach churned with fear. He'd promised Hope he would find her brother. He couldn't let her down.

Riding into his yard, he climbed down from his horse and undid the saddle. The poor thing had been with him most of the night after he'd let the one he'd used all day have a rest. He was going to just go inside and splash some cool water on his face before saddling up another one to go back out.

He was supposed to check back in at his mother's at daybreak. He only hoped one of the others had been lucky enough to find the boy. Opening the door to his small house, he moved to the table to light the lantern and dispel the dark shadows in the room.

He pulled his hat from his head and pushed his fingers through his hair. His whole body was tired, and all he wanted was to go crawl into his bed and sleep for days. But he couldn't. He had to find Max.

Going to the small washstand he had in the corner of the room, he bent down and splashed the water on his face. As he rubbed his hands down his cheeks, he could feel the stubble that had already started to grow back. It had felt good to shave yesterday after months on the trail, but that smoothness was no longer there.

Deciding he'd go and change his shirt, he started to unbutton the one he wore as he walked into the room behind the fireplace. Stopping dead in his tracks, the air left his lungs as he saw the small body curled up sleeping peacefully on his bed.

This whole time, while they'd been out looking everywhere for him, Max had been sound asleep at his place. Logan had come inside a couple of times while they searched, but he hadn't gone into the bedroom, never imagining the boy would have simply gone there to hide.

Logan honestly didn't know whether to laugh with joy, or cry at the amount of time they'd all wasted looking.

Max rolled over and opened his eyes. He looked scared for a moment, until he realized where he was. He sat up and rubbed at his eyes.

Logan sat down on the edge of the bed and pulled him in for a hug. He couldn't be angry at the boy for being scared and thinking he needed to run. But he was going to make sure Hope told him not to do this anymore.

Logan signed to him and told him he was taking him to his sister. Max nodded sheepishly.

Saddling up a fresh horse, he put the boy in

front of him and raced to his mother's. He knew Hope hadn't slept all night, coming to the doorway every time she'd heard them ride into the yard.

But this time, as he watched her come to the doorway, his chest burst with happiness to see her face light up with joy.

Riding up beside the house, he helped Max dismount into Hope's waiting arms. His mother had come out behind Hope, and beamed up at Logan.

He climbed down and was almost knocked off balance before his feet hit the ground. Hope flung herself into his arms, leaving him no choice but to wrap his around her waist. His eyes met his mother's over the top of Hope's head, and she winked as she took Max's hand, leading him inside the house.

"Thank you, Logan." Her words were muffled in his chest. Gently pressing on her shoulders, he pushed her back to look down into her tear-streaked face. "It seems like that's all I'm ever saying to you. You've had to constantly rescue me or my brother since the day you met us. I'm sure you're wishing you'd just let Max run away with your wallet that day."

His hand came up to brush the hair from her

eyes. "No, I thank the good Lord every day I followed Max. He led me to you."

Before she could respond, the sound of hoof-beats coming up the road broke the silence. Letting his arms drop, he stepped back before anyone saw them. Even though he had full intentions of letting Hope know his feelings, that would have to wait.

As the others came into the yard, and were filled in on where Max had been found, his eyes stayed on Hope. He knew the hardest part was about to come.

Today, Sadie was showing up in town, and he still didn't know how he was going to stop her from taking Max from them.

All he knew was, she was going to have to go through him first.

CHAPTER 19

They stood outside the mercantile, listening to Susan O'Hara fussing over Max as she took him inside, chattering away as though he could hear every word she said. To his credit, Max had taken an instant liking to the older woman, and was more than happy to let her dote on him. Plus, the fact she was offering him candy didn't hurt either.

The family had ridden in early this morning, determined to be ready to meet Sadie as soon as she arrived. They were ready to show her they weren't backing down, and if she thought she was just going to ride away with Max, she was going to have a fight on her hands first.

Hope nervously wrung her hands together, still not sure this was the best idea. Her instinct had been to take Max and get as far away from here as she could. But like Logan had said, she would have to be prepared to spend the rest of her life running and always looking over her shoulder to see if someone was coming to take Max.

He'd assured her that he wouldn't let Sadie win, and she had no reason not to believe him. Ever since the day he'd seen her at the auction, he'd come through for her. He'd been the one person in her life she knew she could trust and count on.

Well, she guessed now, that also included his entire family. She had never met people so fiercely loyal and ready to stand up and help a stranger. It was the kind of family she'd always dreamed of having.

Reminding herself they weren't her family, and she still didn't know if she'd even be staying after this was all over, she ignored the feeling of sadness that crept in at that thought.

Clarence and his men were standing guard across the street near the stagecoach stop. Every time she saw him sitting on the bench, booted foot resting on his other knee as he leaned back and relaxed, she wanted to run over and slap him.

She was on edge, and every sound or movement near her made her jump. Phoebe and Audrey sat with her in the wagon, while the men walked around discussing what their plan would be if anything went wrong.

Titus had been charged with grabbing Max and riding as fast as he could away from here, while the others would deal with Sadie and the thugs. Hope couldn't listen anymore, worry over any of them getting hurt because of her and Max was eating at her soul. She'd never wanted to drag anyone into her problems, and now here they were, waiting to confront the woman who was evil enough to sell her stepdaughter at an auction without feeling a twinge of remorse.

Ella came over and hopped up into the wagon. She was wearing her "work" clothes that she wore while working with the horses, so she didn't have the heavy skirts to hinder her movements. "Max is happily sitting behind the counter with Susan enjoying a piece of hard candy." She sat down next to Hope, reaching over and squeezing her hand.

Just then, the sound of a stagecoach could be heard coming around the corner into town. The steady clip-clop of the horse's hooves seemed to echo her pulse as it pounded in her ears.

Logan's eyes met hers, and he came to the back of the wagon, putting his hand out to help her down. When she got to the end of the box, he reached both hands up and lifted her down. Setting her on the ground, he held her in front of him, his hands still firmly around her waist as he looked down at her.

"Do you trust me?"

She nodded, knowing her heart truly did trust him. Somehow she just knew in that moment, Sadie wasn't going to win.

He stepped back, pulling her to his side as his hand found hers. They stood waiting for the stagecoach to stop, while Clarence and his men walked to greet the occupants.

Sadie stepped out in a flurry of silk skirts, her head looking around in disdain at the dusty town she'd arrived in. Spotting Hope, she immediately made her way over. "Well, if it isn't my dear step-daughter waiting to greet me." The words came out as a sneer as Sadie twisted her lip up in obvious disgust as she looked Hope up and down. "I see the auction didn't turn out too badly for you."

Hope swallowed hard. "No, Sadie, in fact, I should probably thank you. You sending me to that auction was the best thing that's ever happened to me."

She enjoyed seeing the look of fury on her stepmother's face. She hadn't cared what happened to Hope after the auction, and had even seemed to be wishing the worst possible outcome for her. So knowing her plan hadn't worked out wouldn't make her happy.

A man had stepped out of the stagecoach behind Sadie, and walked over to stand next to her. "Mr. Daniels?" Sadie's lawyer had come with her. Maybe now Hope could get some answers.

Sadie was grinning at her as she reached out and wrapped her arms around his. Hope looked back and forth between them, and she realized there was something more between them. As she thought back, she remembered that Mr. Daniels had seemed to be around the house an awful lot, and now she wondered if there had been more than a professional reason for him to be there.

"We're here to get Max, Hope. And, the papers I have here indicate there is nothing you can do to stop us. Sadie is Max's legal guardian."

"I'm eighteen now. I can be his guardian."

Mr. Daniels shook his head. "No, I'm afraid your father's will was very specific in wanting Max to remain in Sadie's care until the boy is of age himself."

Hope could feel herself start to shake. She

knew they should have got away from here while they could. But Logan squeezed her hand, reassuring her that he wasn't going to just give up.

"What I don't understand is, if you were so eager to ship the boy off to an orphanage while you were selling your stepdaughter to the highest bidder, why are you so intent on getting your hands on him now? Why do you care so much now?" Logan's voice rumbled loudly beside her.

"Maybe my undying love for the boy has been realized." Sadie laughed sadistically as she shrugged. "Whatever my reasons, they're no concern of you. I'm taking Max with me, and there's nothing you can do to stop me."

Clarence stepped forward slightly, obviously ready for a fight.

Suddenly, hooves pounding the ground could be heard coming into town. Hope turned her head, seeing two riders on horseback flying toward them with a cloud of dust in their wake. As they rode up beside them on the street, Hope's mouth opened in surprise.

"Camille?" She could barely get her voice out as she struggled to make sense out of what was happening. Why was her best friend from Sacramento here?

Her friend's horse had barely come to a stop before the woman had jumped down beside Hope. She was dressed much the same as Ella was today, wearing pants and a shirt that Hope was sure must belong to a man.

"What are you doing here?"

Nothing was making sense.

Her friend came over and stood by her. "Because I thought you might like to hear the truth about your father's will, Hope. And why your charming stepmother here was so eager to sell you off to the highest bidder."

"But how...why—?"

Camille gave her a quick hug, then pulled back to smile at her. "Hope, I want you to know that my friendship with you has always been true. But I wasn't entirely honest with you about who I was. My name is actually Myra Dixon, and I'm a Pinkerton agent."

CHAPTER 20

*H*ope stood in shock as she listened to her friend fill everyone in on the truth. "When Logan contacted the authorities back in Sacramento about the auction, and let them know he felt there was something else going on with Sadie, one of the agents in the office contacted me. I'd been working undercover for a while now to get information about the illegal auctions happening in town."

"But when did Logan contact anyone?" She looked at Logan, who was still standing beside her. He'd been just as shocked when Camille...no, Myra, had ridden into town and announced herself as an agent. His mouth still hung partway open as he looked at the woman.

"When I went into town to pick up your clothes and other supplies, I didn't trust Sadie or what had been put in the will, and something just wasn't sitting right with me."

Myra pulled out a piece of paper and handed it to Hope. She quickly looked it over, anger boiling inside her as she realized what her stepmother had tried to do. Lifting her head, she met Sadie's eyes as she held the paper up in front of her.

"It would appear this is the true will belonging to my father. And not the made up one you and your friend put together to suit you. You honestly didn't think I'd ever find out, did you?"

Sadie wasn't looking so smug now, her skin had gone a pasty shade of green.

"My father hadn't left us destitute at all. But he had left *you* without any money. My money would become mine as soon as I reached the age of eighteen, and Max would have enough money put away for him to go to his legal guardian to ensure he was well taken care of for the rest of his life. And that legal guardian was to be me as soon as I reached the age of eighteen." She was shaking with anger now as she realized the full extent of what Sadie had planned to do.

Myra moved closer to Sadie, and as Clarence

and his men started to back up slightly, the other agent who'd been with Myra went to stand by them.

"If something happened to you, and you didn't collect your inheritance, it would then go to Sadie. But for Max, the guardian had to take him into your father's lawyer's office to collect. Without Max, no money could be dispersed." Myra finished the rest of it for her.

Sadie shook her head and laughed. "Well, you might think you've won, Hope Saunders. But you've just ensured your brother will go to an orphanage after all. Because in case you didn't read the fine print on that document, the only way Max will go to you after the age of eighteen is if you're married. Obviously your father didn't think you could manage to look after a deaf boy on your own."

Hope looked back down, her eyes scanning the paper to see if Sadie was right. Her stomach sunk as she saw the words. How could she have missed that part?

"And since these Pinkerton agents are bound to uphold the law, I guess they'll be required to take Max with them when they return to Sacramento."

After all this, everything she'd been through,

and finding out the truth about it all, she was still going to lose her brother.

Her knees started to give out, but Logan's arm wrapped itself around her waist, pulling her into his side.

"No, Max won't be going anywhere," Logan spoke up as he pinned his gaze on Sadie's.

"Because Hope will be marrying me."

~

"Logan, you don't have to do this. You've already had to do more than you should have. I can't ask you to marry me just so I can keep Max."

"I'm not just marrying you so you can keep Max."

Her mind was spinning with everything she'd just found out and she was having a hard time understanding what he was saying. She looked back to the mercantile where Myra and her partner were tying the hands of Sadie and Mr. Daniels. Clarence and his men were still standing there, but so far, it didn't look like they were being arrested.

Logan had practically dragged her over here

after his announcement, while she'd been standing and staring at him in shock.

His blue eyes held hers when she turned back to look at him.

"You've already had to do so much. Ever since you walked into that tavern, you've been stuck with me and Max, having to do everything to keep us safe. You never asked for any of it, and now that I have the money, I can pay you back. I can take care of Max now, so you can finally be free of us."

"You heard what she said, Hope. You don't get legal guardianship unless you're married."

She closed her eyes briefly, wishing she could just have a minute to process everything she'd just found out.

"I can't ask you to do that for me." Her voice was pained as she spoke.

Logan lifted his hand and brushed the tear from her cheek that was slowly making its way down. "Hope, I'm not just doing it for you. I'm doing it for Max. And I'm doing it for me."

His thumb made circles on her cheek as he continued. "Ever since the moment I saw you standing on that platform, you've had my heart. I was just too stubborn to admit it. So yes, I'm marrying you so you can stop having to run and worry about someone taking your brother from you. But, I'm also doing it because I can't imagine my life without you in it."

Her lips parted, but she didn't know what to say. Her heart soared, and the tears she'd been crying a moment before turned to tears of happiness.

"I love you, Hope. And I'd like to have the chance to spend my life with you, and with Max."

"I love you too, Logan. I've never known a man who would so selflessly help a complete stranger, and be someone she could always count on from the moment they met. You've done more than you ever had to do, and I know I could never repay you."

He shook his head and laughed quietly. "Can't you see, Hope? You've already paid me back more than I ever needed."

He brought his lips down to hers, pulling her in closer as he brought his hand up and caressed the back of her neck. She clung to him, never wanting to let go. She groaned as he finally pulled back, and he smiled down into her upturned face.

"Does that mean you'll marry me?"

She laughed and shrugged. "Aren't you afraid it'll make you soft?"

With a grin, he nodded. "It sure is funny what a woman can do to a man."

EPILOGUE

$\mathcal{T}$he water trickled over the rocks, the gentle sound reaching her ears as she leaned back in Logan's arms. They sat leaning against a tree, watching Max chase Sophia, who would squeal with laughter as he pretended he couldn't keep up.

The family had ridden out to Reid and Audrey's for the Sunday picnic they hadn't been able to have last week.

As Hope thought about the events of the last week, she was sure she'd dreamed most of it. When Logan had told her he loved her, and that he wanted to marry her for reasons other than just to protect Max, her heart had soared.

And he hadn't wasted any time. He said he

wasn't giving anyone the chance to get their hands on Max, and had insisted they be married that day.

She was still in shock about finding out Camille was actually a Pinkerton agent named Myra. Every time she thought back to when she'd met Camille, and the time they'd spent together, she realized her friend had never really given her much information about her life or where she'd come from.

But, Myra—as Hope was trying to remember to call her—had assured her their friendship was real, and she'd been devastated to hear that Hope had been put through one of the illegal auctions she was hired to stop.

Myra and her partner had taken Sadie and Mr. Daniels back to Sacramento to face their charges. Clarence and his men were let go since they really hadn't done anything illegal, other than threaten them. When he'd discovered he wasn't getting paid after the weeks he'd wasted, he was angry.

Logan had said he wouldn't want to be Sadie when she got out of prison because Clarence wasn't someone who'd just go away when he was owed money.

Letting herself relax against Logan's chest, she took in the beauty around her. The breeze kissed her skin as they sat in the shade of the branches overhead. His arms held her tightly, pulling her back against him. His chest moved as he breathed, and she could feel the steady beating of his heart against her back.

Her eyes closed as his fingers began to trail along the skin on her arm, moving slowly up and down.

"Max has sure settled in well here. It's been nice to see him get the chance to be a kid and know he has a place where he can't ever be taken away from."

His chest rumbled as he spoke, making her open her eyes back up and focus on Max.

"Yes, he told me you've already learned more to be able to talk with him than our father ever did in all his life. I don't think he could ever understand why his own father didn't care to communicate with him. I think deep down, he knew what a disappointment he was, so he mostly just spent his days staying out of his way."

"I think your father likely cared about him. That was evident by how he made sure his son would always be cared for after he was gone. He just didn't know how to deal with a child that required the special care Max did. I'm not saying what he did was right, but sometimes people do things they regret and don't know how to make them right again. The fact that Sadie got nothing unless there was no one else to get the money shows that he may have realized the woman he married wasn't quite the best choice for his children."

Hope smiled to herself, knowing his words were true. Their father had been a good man who lost his way after he felt like he'd failed his son.

"Are you two trying to hide from the rest of us over here?" Luke laughed to himself as he sat down on the ground beside them. Logan groaned loudly at the intrusion.

But before he could reply, Ella and Titus came over, and Hope put her arms out to take the baby. Looking down into the sleeping face of the little girl with blonde hair covering her head, Hope smiled. "My goodness, little Rose, you sure do look like your mama."

The mule named Wally who seemed to follow Ella and Titus everywhere—even riding in the wagon and going to visit family for Sunday lunches—ambled over and started rummaging in the bush behind them.

The others all came over too, sitting down to

rest under the shade of the tree. Hope looked around at these people—the Wallace's—who'd welcomed both her and her brother into their family. They'd opened their homes and their hearts to them, and accepted them with open arms. And there was Luke Hamilton, who'd always been ready to do what was needed to keep her safe, without question or complaint.

Her eyes found James and Susan O'Hara. They'd become dear to her too, and she knew without a doubt they were two people who would do anything for the people they cared about.

And of course, the man who held her in his arms. He'd walked into a dingy tavern to retrieve his property and ended up saving her life. She couldn't bear to think what would have happened to her if she hadn't seen those bright, blue eyes staring at her across the room.

She'd sworn to pay him back for everything he'd done for her, and now, she knew she'd spend the rest of her life doing just that.

"You know, Logan, if I didn't know any better, I'd be almost certain you were getting soft."

Hope laughed softly as Colton spoke.

She felt his shoulders move behind her as he lifted them.

"Well, if it means I get to spend the rest of my life with Hope in my arms, then I guess that's exactly what I am."

Max ran over and sat on the ground beside them, grinning up at Logan as he moved his hands to speak. Hope's heart filled with happiness as Logan replied, carefully moving his hands to make sure he got it right.

"What did he say?" Luke had been trying to learn some of the words, as had everyone else, but they still weren't able to understand everything.

Logan reached out and pulled Max over beside him, holding his arm around him as he hugged him in close too.

"He said, '*I love it here. Thank you for not letting them take me away.*'"

Hope decided to tell them all what Logan had replied.

"And Logan has told him no one will ever take him away, because now this is his home."

Her chest ached with happiness, sitting here with everyone she loved, knowing they truly had found home.

∽

I HOPE that you enjoyed reading Hope's Honor. If you could take a moment to head back to where you bought it and leave a review, it would be very much appreciated :)

ABOUT THE AUTHOR

Kay P. Dawson is a stay at home mom of two girls, who always dreamed of being a writer. After a breast cancer diagnosis in 2011, she decided it was time to follow her dream.

Years of reading historical romance, combined with her love for all history related to the old west and pioneer times, she knew that writing in the western historical genre was her calling.

She writes sweet romance, believing a good love story doesn't need to give all of the juicy details - a true love story shows so much more.

~

**I have a Facebook fan group set up for anyone who enjoys my books, and reading in the sweet western romance genre - and I would love to have you join us! There are special giveaways and fun events just for members...and a place just to hang out with others :)

You can join at: https://www.facebook.-com/groups/kaypdawsonfans/

Newsletter SignUp:
http://www.kaypdawson.com/newsletter

Don't forget to follow me on Bookbub - you will get all new release special deal alerts!
https://www.bookbub.com/authors/kay-p-dawson

kaypdawson.com
kaypdawsonwrites@gmail.com